PROMISES

SUN VALLEY SERIES, BOOK 4

KELLIE COATES GILBERT

Dedicated to Lynne Gentry, a fellow author I talk with nearly every morning. We've walked this publication journey together for over ten years. I am blessed to call her my friend.

PRAISE FOR KELLIE COATES GILBERT

"If you're looking for a new author to read, you can't go wrong with Kellie Coates Gilbert."
~**Lisa Wingate**, NY Times bestselling author of *Before We Were Yours*

"Well-drawn, sympathetic characters and graceful language"
~**Library Journal**

"Deft, crisp storytelling"
~**RT Book Reviews**

"I devoured the book in one sitting."
~**Chick Lit Central**

"Gilbert's heartfelt fiction is always a pleasure to read."
~**Buzzing About Books**

"Kellie Coates Gilbert delivers emotionally gripping plots and authentic characters."
~**Life Is Story**

"I laughed, I cried, I wanted to throw my book against the wall, but I couldn't quit reading."
~**Amazon reader**

"I have read other books I had a hard time putting down, but this story totally captivated me."
~**Goodreads reader**

"I became somewhat depressed when the story actually ended. I wanted more."

~Barnes and Noble reader

ALSO BY KELLIE COATES GILBERT

Mother of Pearl

Sisters (Sun Valley Series Book 1)

Heartbeats (Sun Valley Series Book 2)

Changes (Sun Valley Series Book 3)

Promises (Sun Valley Series Book 4)

Otherwise Engaged – a Love on Vacation Story

All Fore Love – a Love on Vacation Story

A Woman of Fortune - Texas Gold Book 1

Where Rivers Part - Texas Gold Book 2

A Reason to Stay - Texas Gold Book 3

What Matters Most - Texas Gold Book 4

More information and purchase links can be found at:

www.kelliecoatesgilbert.com

*

"**L**adies and gentlemen, as we start our descent, please make sure your seat backs and tray tables are in their full upright position. Your seat belt should be securely fastened and stow all carry-on luggage securely underneath the seat in front of you or in the overhead bins. Thank you.*"*

As always, Karyn Macadam did as she was told. She handed off her empty coffee cup to the flight attendant who was making one final stroll down the aisle. They granted each other the obligatory smile before Karyn turned and peered out the window at the familiar landscape below. A wintery blanket of white with ribbons of icy blue rivers spanned as far as she could see. In the far distance, jagged snow-covered mountains jutted from the horizon against a pale white sky—the color of wedding dresses.

She hated weddings.

Okay, hate was a strong word. Yet, the strong emotion seemed perfectly appropriate. She liked the concept that relationships end happily-ever-after. Unfortunately, she'd learned you couldn't count on that adage to always be true.

Still, she'd do anything for her sister. Even if it meant swallowing her own melancholy in order to celebrate Joie's special day.

Her seat mate, who had thankfully slept most of the flight, perked up, tilted her head slightly, as if she was noticing Karyn for the first time. "Excuse me, but you look very familiar." She looked thoughtful for a moment. "I'm sure I know you from somewhere."

Karyn cringed. She'd almost made the entire trip without the familiar exchange.

"Yes, I'm sure I've seen you before." The older woman, dressed in tailored slacks, a turtle-necked sweater with her hair tucked up in a gray felt wool fedora—designer—leaned uncomfortably close. "I never forget a face."

Karyn nervously picked a tiny piece of lint from her black pants, thankful the flight was nearly over. The last thing she wanted was to carry on a hollow conversation with some stranger, especially a woman who did not respect personal space.

The woman's forefinger flew up. "I remember where I know you from! You're that gal who was in all the newspapers after her husband died up here on the mountain. Such a tragic story. My, you were so poised in the aftermath."

Karyn drew a calming breath, tried to stay pleasant. "Thank you."

The woman tightened her seat belt. "I'm so glad I was able to recall how I recognized you. That would have plagued me, even kept me awake. I certainly couldn't afford that." She leaned in so close, Karyn could smell her breath mint. "I have a full agenda while here in Sun Valley and will need all my sleep."

Karyn squirmed in her seat, leaned back a bit, waiting for the plane's descent.

The woman moved, closing the distance Karyn had created. "There's supposed to be a big storm coming in from the Pacific.

I was a tad afraid I might not make it in before it hit, so I came in a few days early."

Finally, the plane's nose dipped. The landing gear descended.

The woman clasped the arms of her seat. "I'm reluctant to admit this, but I hate landings. I don't mind take-offs, but landings . . . " She visibly shuddered, squeezed her eyes shut.

"Yes, landings can be rocky," Karyn said, with a barely audible sigh of resignation. In the distance, she spotted the Friedman Memorial terminal and the familiar hangar where Grayson had kept his airplane—the place where she and Grayson had enjoyed a special picnic before climbing aboard his Cessna and going for a flight across the Wood River Valley. That day was a turning point in their budding friendship—the first time she'd risked her heart since losing her husband.

It had never entered her mind to brace herself for yet another loss.

She gripped the armrests, waited for the moment of touchdown, held her breath as the fuselage shifted a bit on the recently plowed runway.

Inside the terminal, Karyn hurried to gather her bags.

The lady from the plane lugged her suitcase off the turnstile. "Well, it was nice meeting you."

Karyn nodded politely. "Yeah, same."

She headed for the door leading to long term parking, quickly moving past the exact spot where everything had changed that day.

How could she have known Grayson's ex-wife would show up and entice him back to Alaska to play daddy to an adorable toddler—leaving her to wonder how she would survive his leaving?

Zane Keppner had been a huge factor in her getting her feet back on solid ground. His no-nonsense style had been good for her. He'd forced her to take ownership of her own happiness, helped her stretch and take chances. Like following him to California.

Leaving her home, her new job at the Sun Valley Lodge, even if temporarily, had felt a bit like jumping off a cliff in freefall. A move that was far more consistent with Joie's style, not hers.

Her oldest sister, Leigh Ann, had tried to talk her out of it. "I know this Kepper's photos have been featured in every food magazine in the country, but you don't even know this guy," she'd cautioned, not able to hide the horror on her face after learning the news. "You can't just leave and wander around California with some stranger. No sane person does that."

But she had.

With luggage in tow, Karyn pushed through the double glass doors and stepped into the frigid temperatures, tightening her scarf.

In many ways, the decision was the best she'd made in years. She'd been able to shed the looks of pity from everyone who knew her, instead embarking on an adventure unlike anything she'd ever known.

She'd traveled with Dean when he was on the Olympic circuit. But that was different.

This time . . . Well, this time she'd enjoyed the freedom to explore what she wanted to see, eat what she wanted to taste. The sounds seemed more resonant, the sights more vivid. Zane made sure of it. He'd pushed her to unshackle the weight she carried—the heavy burden of pleasing everyone around her. These months had taught her to enjoy the little things—and she'd learned to genuinely smile again.

She dug her key fob out of her purse, pressed the button. The rear door to her SUV opened and she lifted her bag into the back.

No doubt, Sun Valley was her home. So many of her memories were tucked within the folds of the growing Idaho resort town. With eyes closed, she could imagine every street corner, every building. Her dad, her sisters, so many lifetime friends were anchors for her heart.

Even so, after much thought she'd realized clinging to the past, staying safe and comfortable, was no longer in her best interest.

Another turning point stood in her path—one that would impact not only her, but would ripple through her family and friends. Despite potential pushback, she'd made a critical decision. Her next move would change everything.

2

Leigh Ann Blackburn burst through the doors leading to the Painted Lady Art Studio just as the proprietor, Trudy Dilworth, was wrapping up her class.

"Oh, excuse me!" Leigh Ann said, sorry for her intrusion.

Miss Trudy waved her ample arm, sending the sleeve of her brightly-colored caftan flowing. "No worries, dear." Her bracelets jangled as she turned her attention to her students. "Let's practice our strokes. Remember, watercolor painting is not about control. It's about letting go!" She rewarded those sitting in front of their easels with a confident smile. "Just let go."

She peeked over the shoulder of Rene Cole, a woman with white hair and bright pink lips. Mrs. Cole had recently retired from the Mountain Express, where she'd written the obituary column for over forty years. "That's right, Rene. Perfect!" Miss Trudy gave her a pat on the back before waving Leigh Ann towards her office in the back.

"Oh, Miss Trudy. I'm so sorry. I didn't mean to interrupt." Leigh Ann pulled her wool scarf from around her neck, scrunched her nose against the smell of turpentine and paint.

"I dropped by to check on Joie's gifts for her bridesmaids. To see how they're coming along."

"Oh yes, dear. They're finished. The charms turned out just like we'd hoped. Come see!"

The trinkets were indeed everything she'd hoped for—and then some. Miss Trudy was a woman of many talents. None could surpass her ability to create stunning one-of-a-kind jewelry pieces.

"I had some great help," Miss Trudy confided. "I hired a talented intern a while back. Her name is Lindsay."

Leigh Ann nodded. "Oh, yes. Jess Barnett's new wife. He's our sous chef at the lodge."

"That's right. I nearly forgot he works with you. Such a sweet couple, those two." Miss Trudy went to work placing the charms in individual cream-colored satin bags with gold ties—Joie's wedding colors. "Anyway, Lindsay made something similar for her own wedding. Earrings with little aquamarine stones. They were a big hit. I know these will be too."

Leigh Ann hoped Joie agreed. She'd stopped next door at the law firm to see if her younger sister had time to venture over to take a peek with her, but learned she was in a client meeting. Truth was, Joie always seemed to be in a meeting, or otherwise unavailable. It was as if she was completely disinterested in her own wedding. Leigh Ann had accused her of as much.

Joie simply rolled her eyes in response. "You know I hate stuff like this."

"This is your *wedding*, Joie. I mean, c'mon—"

"Which is quickly becoming a circus."

The comment stung. "Oh, so now I'm turning your wedding into a circus?"

Joie immediately softened. "You're misunderstanding what I'm trying to say—"

"Because you can pick up your own dress from the seamstress. You can call the caterers and figure out what appetizer to serve. You can negotiate with the harpist regarding when she'll show up and tell the florist we don't want her to use any orchids because they always wilt too quickly."

"Oh, don't go all drama on me. We both know you have no plans to use a caterer. Amelio and his kitchen staff at the lodge are providing all the food and you've spend glorious hours huddled over coffee with your friend at the nursery picking every stinking bloom." She held up open palms. "It's not that I don't appreciate everything you've done. I do. But I told you when all this began I'd consent to you running everything because I simply didn't have time. Frankly, a quiet ceremony at the church, or out at Dad's would suit me just fine."

Leigh Ann waved her off. "Yeah? And what are you going to tell your high school biology teacher and his wife when they call and ask about why they weren't invited to the ceremony? How about Nelly, the librarian, or Nash Billingsley and Lucy down at Bistro on Fourth? Are you willing to crush all their feelings by not including them in the most important night of your life?"

Joie rubbed her forehead in frustration. "We already had this conversation."

True. Leigh Ann had known at that point in their earlier conversation Joie was beginning to fold. Still, she'd played the Mom card as insurance. "I'm pretty sure our mother would have wanted her baby girl to put her nuptials front and center, not leave anyone out."

Whether Joie had backed down because of that sentimental notion, or she'd simply grown tired of arguing, it didn't matter. She'd given in and consented to the whole notion. The ceremony at the church, the sleigh ride to the Sun Valley Lodge where there would be a huge reception, including a sit-down dinner for four hundred. Joie's wedding celebration would be the showcase of Sun Valley.

As always, in the end, Joie would thank her. Her special night would be a night to look back upon with fond memories.

Finished with the task of bagging the gifts, Miss Trudy now turned and echoed the same sentiment. "This wedding is certainly going to be a night to remember."

JOIE ABBOTT BENT and checked the bindings on her skis, then straightened to survey the landscape before her. For days, the skies over Sun Valley had been gray with the threat of more snow. Early this morning, the sun broke through the clouds—a clear invite for Joie to rearrange her office schedule so she could head up the mountain and clear her mind.

She stabbed her poles into the thin frozen crust and drew a deep breath. Once, she'd read a magazine article while in a dentist's waiting room that explained how cold weather slows down molecules in the air, and with less molecular activity, certain smells become less pungent. That means "smelling snow" is, in part, just smelling fewer odors outdoors than what you're used to.

That theory was bunk in her mind.

Snow, especially freshly-fallen snow, had a definite smell. The smell of clear, fresh freedom—and she needed some clarity right now, and to be free of the junk circling her head. Which is why she'd escaped the office. Why she'd told Margaret Adele to explain she was in a meeting and couldn't be interrupted if anyone showed up. And by anyone, she meant her sister who had become obsessed with wedding plans.

The first run had been fairly easy, one meant for medium skill level. But this course would take every ounce of her expertise. Her eyesight blurred slightly. She began to hyperventilate, and her calves shook as she basked in the thrill she knew was coming.

She gazed at the steep drop, the glittering white blanket bordered by pine trees, their spidery branches heavily laden with ice.

Joie tightened her grip on the pole handles and shoved off. She hurtled down the groomed fall line at breakneck speed in the direction of a natural lift. Hitting her target, she felt herself go airborne for several seconds before dropping several feet, plummeting back to the snowline, diverting into a deeper area that had not been groomed.

Instantly, all was lost from view. Everything disappeared— the sky, the trees, and even her hands were suddenly hidden in a sea of white. The powder was deeper than anything she'd experienced, and for a second she couldn't tell if she were moving or if she'd stalled in a snowdrift.

Seconds later, she felt her legs beneath her, her skis flying on autopilot. Two turns, then three—all under a blanket of frozen white until she gained enough momentum to broach the surface. And not a moment too soon as a wave of airborne powder flew over her helmet.

Her heart raced with exhilaration.

It was true—skiing pow was like swimming through a white sea. You're in it, and it's in you.

Joie hooted with giddiness.

Suddenly, her skis broke through and she landed on corduroy—snow that had been groomed leaving tiny grooves that resembled its namesake fabric.

She picked up speed, raced down the slope.

Swish—glide—swish!

She could feel her dad's presence, hear him egg her on. *"Sit back on the tails of your skis, sweetheart. It'll give you much better balance and stability."*

This was what she'd so missed—the closest feeling to flying she'd experienced in a long while. And especially since all this silly wedding business had begun.

She'd wanted something on a lot less grand scale. Yet, it had soon grown tedious defending her desire for something small, intimate. Against her better judgment, she'd finally given in to the pressure that seemed to come at her from multiple directions. Even Clint had reminded her that people just wanted to share their joy.

Unfortunately, just like she'd imagined, the plans had taken on a life of their own, like an overgrown garden that becomes so dense and unwieldy, you can no longer see the blooms. Frankly, she couldn't wait to view the entire episode in life's rearview mirror. All she wanted was to be Mrs. Clint Ladner and be done.

Pushing the negative thoughts from her mind, Joie focused back on her run. She didn't want to think about any of that now. Not while she was on the mountain. Instead, she lengthened her turns, swinging broad and wide, letting the sun warm her face and her soul.

Several yards later, she hit another change in the snow surface. As predicted in the morning's snow report, the corduroy turned to crud which made her work harder to maintain her speed and balance. She gripped the poles tighter, pushed against the skis' surface a little harder, made tighter turns.

Joie crossed the lane, veered dangerously close to the tree line. She laughed out loud as she tucked and gained speed, straightening seconds before she hit another pile of snow that launched her airborne.

Joie glided through the air in what seemed like slow motion and landed without wavering.

For the next minutes, everything in the world was right. Far before she was ready, the run was over. She plowed to a stop at the base of Olympic Ridge.

Joie couldn't help herself as she rose from unhooking the bindings and stepped from her skis. She let her poles drop and flung her arms in the air.

"Whoo hoo! That was great!"

3

J oie pulled her new Jeep Cherokee, one with proper fastening mechanisms for Hudson's car seat, into the driveway of what would soon be her home.

The house was a newly built two-story made of raw timber with lots of glass—a modern architecture that wasn't fussy. Her father had surprised her and Clint with the gift of a plot of land—a parcel carved from the ranch. He'd also helped them secure the necessary financing for the build-out. In addition to his duties at the stables, Clint was serving as the general contractor, which had saved them a significant amount of money.

While she was grateful, the financial commitment made her nervous. Her law practice was still fairly new, and Clint's salary had its limits. Besides, a thirty-year mortgage? Well, thirty years was a long time. Almost more than she could comprehend. She often didn't know what tomorrow would bring. How could she know this is where she wanted to live for the next thirty years?

Falling in love with Clint Ladner was everything Joie had dreamed it would be. In fact, she'd been in love with him far longer than she allowed herself to admit. When he got up on the stand in that courtroom last fall and professed his profound regard for her, his unwavering support—well, she could no longer deny how he had painted the landscape of her life with vibrant color.

It had been easy to say yes to his proposal. And she was looking forward to being his wife, to spending the rest of the lives together.

It was this wedding business that had sent her swimming in deep water. That, and all the transition she'd made lately. It wasn't easy to trade in riding Harleys for domesticity.

She parked and climbed from the driver's seat.

Her dad's house was visible in the distance, along with the familiar structures that comprised the ranch compound—the lambing sheds, the cook house, the barns. If she had to put down roots, living so near her father on the ranch she loved was a definite upside. She supposed she needed to dwell on that.

Joie juggled her briefcase with the box of light switches she'd picked up at the hardware store for Clint and moved to shut the car door with her hip.

A familiar voice rang out. "Hey, babe!"

She looked up to find Clint standing in the open doorway, holding little Hudson. Her son spotted her, wiggled his chubby little legs and reached his arms in her direction.

"Hey, you two." She climbed the steps to join them.

"Here, let me help you with that." Clint moved to take the box at the same time she lifted Hudson from his arms.

"How are you, sweet boy?" She kissed the top of her baby's head, nuzzled his hair with her nose. He smelled of baby shampoo, and faintly like sawdust. "Have you been helping with the construction project, big boy?"

Clint pulled her into a brief side hug with his free arm. "Hudson's quite the builder. You should see the way he slams his little rubber hammer against the play pen. With his help, this place will be move-in ready just in time." He tossed the box on the kitchen counter and pulled his phone from his jeans pocket. "Look at this. I took a video."

It warmed her heart that Clint had filled his phone camera with images of Hudson. There were recordings of Hudson splashing the water with his hands while bathing, shots of him sleeping with his dimpled thumb in his mouth, of Hudson's first taste of ice cream. She'd believed no one could love Hudson like her, but clearly Clint walked that line with her shoulder-to-shoulder.

Right after his proposal, Clint urged her to consider letting him adopt Hudson. "Andrew would never allow that. Likely, he's still too angry and dragging his feet on the process to get all this concluded, especially if he knows our plans," she'd gently argued.

"C'mon, it's worth a try. I mean, surely the dude knows you're going to have a life. Hudson needs a dad and he's chosen to bow out of that role. Let me talk to him."

Joie finally agreed. She supposed anything was possible. Andrew hadn't made so much as a move to even see Hudson in the days leading up to the hearing and had agreed to relinquish his parental rights in the aftermath, which proved his attempt to gain full custody had been nothing short of a public relations stunt meant to advance Andrew's political aspirations.

In the end, she'd been wrong about Clint's ability to talk some sense into Andrew.

She placed Hudson down in his Play 'n Pack—tweaked his tiny nose.

To his credit, Andrew gave in and agreed to help clear the way for Clint to make her son his own and expedite the process. This opened the doors to incorporate the adoption proceeding into the wedding celebration. Her law partner, Maddy Crane, had pulled a few strings and arranged for a judge to attend the ceremony and make everything official right after she and Clint were announced as husband and wife. They would walk out of the church not only as husband and wife, but as a family.

"Have you eaten?" Clint asked, his voice pulling her from her reverie. "I have beef stew in the crock pot."

She lifted her eyebrows. "We own a crock pot?"

His face broke into a half smile. "I ordered one online and had it delivered."

"Ah—very resourceful. One more question. Is that thing you're wearing a construction belt, or an apron?" she teased. "And, no, I haven't eaten. I'm starving."

Clint used the only two bowls they currently had in the cupboard and dished up dinner. They wouldn't move in until after the wedding, although Clint had begun sleeping on a cot after putting in late nights.

"You've really made a lot of progress lately," she noted aloud. "I love how everything is coming together."

"Yeah, we've been busy. Luckily, things have been slow at the stables, making it possible to spend the whole day finishing up the molding here in the kitchen. We'll be able to move in right on time."

Joie couldn't help but smile. There was huge comfort in knowing this man would be by her side in the years to come.

"How was your day?" he asked, as he placed her bowl on the table in front of her.

She wasn't sure why, but she was hesitant to tell him she'd skipped out from the office and had gone skiing.

"My day was busy, but fine. It's just—" she said, a little absently. "Oh, never mind. It was fine."

Clint placed his bowl on the table, then moved behind her chair and began rubbing her tight shoulders. "What is it, babe? You can tell me."

She glanced over at Hudson in his Pack 'n Play holding his bottle up all by himself. He was getting so big so quickly.

She turned her attention back to the table, studied the steam rising from her bowl of stew.

"Joie?" Clint kissed the top of her head. Her fiancé was someone who had her number, sometimes before she knew there was a number to be had.

She turned to face him, hating how her eyes threatened to well. "It's nothing really. I'm just under a lot of stress. Work and everything."

Clint had a way of looking past her choices and seeing stuff she didn't always want to show him. How was she supposed to help Clint understand her head game when she didn't fully comprehend the reason for the panicky feelings she'd been having?

Love was supposed to make you feel infinite and invincible, like the whole world was open to you, anything was achievable, and each day filled with wonder. Maybe it was the act of opening yourself up, letting someone else in. Or maybe it was the act of caring so deeply about another person that it expanded your heart.

She never knew how much she could love another human being until she held Hudson in her arms. And now, what she felt for Clint was almost too much to bear. There wasn't enough of her to contain it all. All of this was a bit scary.

She shrugged off the rogue emotion. "Everything is coming at me so fast. And my sister—well, you know how it is with her. To know Leigh Ann is to work for Leigh Ann, whether you voluntarily initiate your employment or not."

Clint chuckled. "That's putting things mildly. Do you want me to talk to her?"

Joie shook her head. "No, I'm just going to let her run with it. The reality is I don't have time to coordinate all the details. I mean, once I folded and agreed to a larger ceremony with all the trappings, I was doomed."

Clint brushed his finger across her cheek. "That's fine to a point. But, this is *our* wedding," he reminded. "If something is important to you, then make sure you say so."

She dismissed his concern with a half-smile that matched the half-truth she was about to tell. "C'mon, Clint. When have you ever known me not to speak my mind?"

4

Leigh Ann turned from her kitchen counter as she heard a car in her driveway. She leaned in to gain a better view. "It's her!" she said out loud to no one but the dog.

She rushed for the front door, flung it open and scrambled for Karyn's car door, instantly wishing she'd taken the time to put on a coat. "There you are," she said, nearly pulling her sister from the front seat.

"Here I am." Karyn climbed out, gave Leigh Ann a tight hug. "Hate to admit it, but I've missed all this snow."

Ignoring the fact she was freezing, Leigh Ann reached in the backseat and pulled out her sister's bag. "Yes, the snow is pretty. Yes, it fuels our economy up here. But, girl! You can't possibly miss the slick roads. And these dropping temperatures are obnoxious."

"Yeah, especially when you're not wearing a coat!" She followed Leigh Ann onto her front porch. "I missed you!" Karyn admitted. "And I've missed Dad and Joie." She stomped the snow from her feet. "Pretty pots."

"Thanks, I filled them with pine and then added aspen

limbs spray painted that glittery silver color. I saw something similar on Pinterest." Leigh Ann took her sister's elbow and guided her inside. "We have to catch up. Tell me everything."

Karyn laughed. "Catch up? We talked on the phone every day. Sometimes twice."

Leigh Ann waved her off. "It's not the same."

Inside, she guided her sister to her guest room. She placed the bag on the end of the bed. "I'm glad you agreed to stay with me instead of holing up alone. After the wedding, we'll work on stocking the refrigerator and cupboards at your house and getting the place ready for you to move back in." She immediately busied herself by unpacking Karyn's bag. She refolded some items and moved for the open bureau drawers. Earlier that morning, she'd tucked little packets of sachet she'd purchased from one of the retail vendors who had come by for their monthly meeting with Paula Martin, the shopkeeper at the Sun Valley Lodge gift shop.

Soon after taking over for Karyn at the Sun Valley Lodge, Leigh Ann had decided she would attend all Paula's meetings with the retailers. She liked to keep her hand on the pulse of every important function at the lodge, and certainly the merchandise selections at the gift shop was something she needed to oversee.

Karyn tried to wedge herself between the open suitcase on the bed and the dresser. "Here, let me do that."

"No, it's nothing. I've got it handled," Leigh Ann insisted. She gave her sister the *look*—the one that said *don't mess with your older sister.*

Karyn shrugged and stepped aside, knowing she had no choice but to give in. "So, where are we having dinner tonight?"

Leigh Ann tucked the final sweater in the top drawer and pushed it closed. "Well, I thought of cooking. Unfortunately, my weekly task list exploded, as you can imagine."

Karyn nodded sympathetically.

"So, I made reservations at the Pioneer."

"I thought you hated the Pioneer, said it's too noisy." She followed Leigh Ann down the hallway and back to the kitchen.

"I do, and it is. But, the Pioneer is also Daddy's favorite. And since he insisted on footing the bill tonight, well . . . " Leigh Ann opened the refrigerator and pulled out two bottles of sparkling water, handing one off to Karyn. "You need to rehydrate. Airplane air sucks you dry."

Karyn unscrewed the top off the bottle. "How's Daddy? I mean, we talk—but it's hard to tell how he's doing from a telephone conversation."

Leigh Ann leaned against the counter, arms folded. "Good. He's good. He won't slow down, of course. In addition to everything he does to manage that ranch, now he's taken on helping with Clint and Joie's house and, well, I only wish he'd realize how old he is and would act it sometimes." She let out a big sigh. "Our only hope is that with Clint living on the ranch, Dad will forfeit some of the responsibility and let his new son-in-law help manage things. Before long, time will sneak up on him and he won't be able to do everything he thinks he can."

Karyn followed Leigh Ann back into the living room. "I don't know," she said. "I'm not sure Dad will ever want to slow down. He's not made that way." She sat on the sofa.

"True," Leigh Ann said, plopping down next to her. She kicked her shoes off and folded her legs up underneath her, just like when they were girls. "Between you and me, I never thought Joie would settle down either—but by this time next week she'll be married and completely established as a wife, mother and lawyer."

"I know there were many occasions when you doubted that coin would ever get tossed." Karyn got a serious look on her face. "How's the wedding plans? Is everything coming together like you'd hoped?"

Leigh Ann ignored how Karyn's voice had grown tentative.

Instead, she let her eyes glisten with excitement. "Oh Karyn, everything is going to be so beautiful. The wedding will be held at the church with Pastor John officiating the ceremony. Right after, a judge will make the adoption official." She swept a piece of lint from the new sofa cushion. "Maddy Crane made that happen, bless her heart."

Finally, Karyn broke into a smile. "That sounds wonderful."

"After the ceremony, there will be a huge reception in the lobby of the Sun Valley Lodge. I've arranged for a surprise appearance by the U.S. Figure Skating Team. They're here in Sun Valley practicing for their winter tour that kicks off in two weeks. Immediately after the ceremony, I'm having them perform on the rink behind the lodge using flares and sparklers. One full-length set with a finale that includes them racing across the ice with a congratulatory banner, then fireworks over the rink."

Karyn raised her eyebrows. "Joie consented to all that?"

Leigh Ann shook her head. "Of course not. It's a surprise!" She clasped her sister's arm with excitement. "And her dress— you should see the dress. I chose it from a line-up of six finalists and finally selected a gorgeous full-length simple A-line styled gown made of satin with a bateau neckline and three-quarter lace sleeves. She'll wear Mom's white fox over-the-shoulder stole while outside. And her long hair will be styled in a messy upsweep with tiny cream buds tucked in the folds."

"Sounds beautiful. And, Joie let you pick everything out?"

Leigh Ann nodded. "I told you, she took her hands completely off. If I hadn't stepped in, just imagine how all this might turn out. Even so, I did everything I could to choose something I knew she wouldn't wig out over. I made every effort to see the selections through her eyes. I personally loved the taffeta full-skirted gown, but knew she'd have a fit over that. Everything I chose is styled simple and elegant with nothing frilly. I really believe she's going to be happy with everything. At least I hope so."

Karyn still looked skeptical. "Well, I'm sure you did your best. What about the color scheme you told me about?"

Leigh Ann clasped her hands. "She didn't argue. Dee Dee ordered plenty of blush-colored roses and peonies, and shell-pink tulips—the lightest shade of pink available. The bridesmaid dresses and groomsmen ties are in the same shades."

Karyn scowled. "I thought Joie had declined having a string of attendants."

Leigh Ann leaned back against the sofa pillows, examined her newly painted toenails. "Well, I pushed a little on that one. It's just you and me up there with her, along with two of her close girlfriends from high school, Pam Curry and Julie Phillips. And Clint's brothers and his best friend are flying in from Texas to stand up with him." She grabbed Karyn's hands in her own. "You'll see. Everything is going to be right out of a bridal magazine."

Karyn couldn't help but smile at her older sister's enthusiasm. No doubt, she loved putting together events, and she was good at it. "Well, let's just hope that predicted storm holds off until after the weekend."

Leigh Ann wasn't concerned. "No worries. We live in a ski resort town. We know how to handle a little snowfall."

The doorbell rang.

Leigh Ann jumped up and hurried to open the door.

"Delivery, ma'am," the young fellow announced in a practiced voice.

Leigh Ann took the bulky packages from his arms and thanked him before shutting the door.

"What's all that?" Karyn asked.

"If I'm lucky, it's the kitten-heeled sandals I ordered for the bridesmaids." She tore open a package and confirmed the contents. "Yes, I'd hoped the shoes would arrive before tomorrow's shower. We're all set now."

She made her way back to the sofa and nestled back into her spot. "So, tell me about California. Was it everything you'd hoped?"

"I told you nearly everything over the phone—"

"Well, yes. We talked on the phone. But I want to know *everything*." Leigh Ann unscrewed the top on her bottle and took a drink.

Karyn quickly shook her head. "I know what you're suggesting and no, Zane and I are still not a thing. We're simply good friends." She smiled. "This is nothing like with Grayson. We really are just good friends."

"Do I need to remind you I've heard that before?" She ignored the look that suddenly crossed Karyn's face, screwed the top back on the bottle. "*Good friends*. What does that even mean?"

"It means that Zane became my confidant, a companion— he was willing to walk through a difficult time in my life. Without any romantic agenda," she emphasized.

Leigh Ann wasn't sure what she thought about that. Could someone who looked like that Keppner guy possibly *not* have some kind of an agenda? She doubted it. "Well, I'm glad you didn't kill yourself on that Harley."

"Oh, I wish you could've seen Glacier National Park—especially from the seat of a bike," Karyn told her. "It's called the Crown of the Continent for a reason."

"Mark and I always intended to take Colby. We just never did, for some reason. Now he's all grown, and well—I guess we should make plans to visit."

"Zane and I made it all the way to West Glacier that first night and stayed in a cute little place that mimicked a building plucked right out of a fifties movie. Gabled door entries and a marquee sign with neon lettering announcing *Vacancy*." She laughed. "Except, one of the letters flashed on and off like there was a short of some sort in the electrical wiring. The lobby even had an old Coca-Cola vending machine with real bottles!"

"Goodness, bottles are so much better than cans. Keeps the soda colder."

"I know, right? Anyway, the next morning we headed out on the bikes for the Going to the Sun Road. The views were breathtaking." She paused, took a drink. "We spent the second night in Great Falls, Montana and then circled down through Yellowstone National Park. Saw a lot of bison and elk, and of course, Old Faithful geyser."

"Remember when Daddy took us there when we were little?"

Karyn nodded. "And Joie pulled away from his hand and ran for the shooting water and Dad had to run after her?" She laughed.

"He had trouble catching her, if I remember correctly."

"She always liked her freedom. And in many ways, I get it. There's not much that compares with heading down the open road on a bike."

Leigh Ann shook her head. "I still can't believe you temporarily left your job, all of us and just took off like that."

Karyn paused. "Yeah, the decision was out of character for me, but I'm so glad I did."

"How did you like Northern California?"

Her sister stared back at her with big, hopeful eyes. "I loved every minute."

Leigh Ann slipped off the couch and headed for the kitchen. "You must've," she called over her shoulder. "I'm still mad at you for not coming home for Thanksgiving or Christmas—or even my annual New Year's Eve party."

"It didn't make sense to come home for your party when it was only weeks to Joie's wedding."

Leigh Ann couldn't hide her scorn. "But the holidays? We always spend the holidays together as a family."

"You want me to see the errors of my ways? Fine, I see the errors. Now, do you plan to pout about that forever?"

Leigh Ann lifted her chin as she tossed the empty bottle in the trash and went for another in the refrigerator. "No, of course not." She let a tiny smile escape her lips. "You're back home now. That's what counts!"

Karyn looked away, drained the remaining sparkling water from her bottle. "You would have loved the wineries in the Napa Valley."

Leigh Ann joined her back on the sofa and handed her a second bottle. "Hydrate," she reminded. "So, Napa Valley is where Zane lives, when he actually stays in one place for a while?"

"He actually resides in Dallas. But he was commissioned to do an extended shoot and so he arranged for a small place in St. Helena. An old friend of his runs a spa and had extra rooms for us to stay in. Grapes aren't the only thing that draws tourists to the Napa Valley, it appears. At the north end of the valley, the high volcanic ash content in the soil has generated another local specialty—therapeutic and rejuvenating mud baths. People flock in from San Francisco and across the country to indulge."

Leigh Ann's eyebrows lifted. "Wait, you're telling me people take a bath in mud? I read an article in a magazine once, but I didn't think normal people actually get in that stuff."

"Oh, yes—and you'd love it."

Leigh Ann continued to look skeptical. "Maybe, but I doubt it. I'm never sinking my body in a bunch of mud that some big 'ole hairy guy just crawled out of."

"Oh, now you're being ridiculous!"

"Am I? Think about it." Leigh Ann bumped her sister's

elbow with her own in a consoling gesture. "Even so, sounds like you really liked the area."

An uncertain gaze shifted onto Karyn's face. "Yes, I really do."

It wasn't until much later that Leigh Ann played the conversation over in her head and realized something she hadn't caught at the time.

Karyn had not used the past tense.

5

The Pioneer Saloon was often the first restaurant tourists headed to when coming into town and the last place to go before leaving. Unlike many of the trendier après-ski locales, the Pioneer, with its interior woodwork, mounted game and period firearms, including Ernest Hemingway's prized 1953 Winchester, Model 21, twelve-gauge shotgun, had an unmatched ambiance that reflected its grand history.

Joie always understood how deeply her father loved the Pioneer. She had experienced his affinity first-hand at the age of eight, when he took her, leaving her two sisters behind, for a daddy/daughter date.

"Dad claimed the Pioneer served the best steaks in all of Idaho," she told Clint as they made their way to the entrance. "He ordered me a ten-ounce sirloin that night, grilled to perfection. I ate the entire thing, and a plate of onion rings, without any coaxing."

He looked up and down her petite frame. "Where'd a little mite like you put all that? In your boots?" His face broke into a wide grin. "I hope I've budgeted enough for groceries."

She punched his arm. "Me? You're the one who can eat a whole pound of bacon for breakfast."

He opened the door. As soon as they entered the restaurant, the owner waved.

"Hey, Duffy," Joie said, as he came over to greet them.

"We've got your family seated," he said, grabbing some menus. "I think you're the last in the party to arrive. Let me take you back." He waved for them to follow. "And congratulations on all the big doings coming up this weekend. Sheila and I are looking forward to it, and we wish you both much happiness."

She thanked him, surprised at how the guest list continued to grow.

Duffy guided them past tables filled with patrons, many chatting loudly while waiting for their meals to be served. Everyone in their dinner party was seated at a large wooden table near the rear.

"There you are!" Leigh Ann wiped her hands on her napkin as she stood. "I was beginning to think you two lovebirds had gotten lost or something."

Joie felt her smile fade. She hated the term lovebirds, especially when used to refer to them. Clint, sensing her displeasure, squeezed her hand in solidarity.

She squeezed back, letting her annoyance fade.

Joie felt everyone's eyes on her. "Sorry, we're late. Hudson was a little fussy after he ate, and we wanted to get him down and asleep before leaving him." She gave her dad a light peck on the cheek. She then turned her attention on Karyn. "Girl, you're looking good. That California air agreed with you."

Karyn stood and drew Joie into a tight embrace. "Missed you, Skunk."

"Isn't it time we drop that moniker?" She didn't need to be reminded that she'd tried to pet what she thought was a kitten all those years ago, only to find out otherwise.

Karyn's eyes sparkled with laughter. "To everyone else,

you'll soon be Mrs. Ladner. But you'll always be our little Skunk."

Joie and Clint greeted everyone else at the table, then slipped into their designated seats. "I hope you don't mind," her dad told them. "We went ahead and ordered some appetizers. Onion rings. Just for you." He gave her a warm smile from the other end of the table.

"You just missed Grandpa's big moment," Colby said. Her nephew exchanged glances with his wife.

"Oh, yes," Nicole confirmed, grinning. "A lady named—" She paused, looked at Colby.

"Elda Vaughn," he inserted.

Nicole quickly nodded. "Yes, Elda Vaughn. Anyway, she came by our table. Put the move on—" She didn't finish the sentence. Instead, she grinned and pointed to Colby's grandpa.

Joie lifted her glass of water from the table, drew it to her mouth. "Oh, Dad. No! Are you kidding? The Bo-Peeps are still after you?" She laughed, then took a drink. Elda was one of many women in town who had romantic intentions towards their father. She and her sisters had nicknamed them the Bo-Peeps and took great glee in teasing him about it.

Her father huffed in response. "I know I'm a catch, but those ladies are going to have to run a whole lot faster. I was in love with one woman, and that was your mother. Not likely to ever happen again."

Before they could argue, a waitress delivered a huge platter of onion rings to the table. Minutes later, their meals arrived. Their father had taken the liberty of ordering steaks all around, huge sirloins grilled to perfection with baked potatoes sporting all the trimmings. "Save room for coconut crème pie," he warned as they were all grabbing for the salt and pepper and bottles of steak sauce.

Clint slipped his arm around Joie. His appreciation for the people around the table could be felt. Clearly, the feeling was mutual. Joie couldn't imagine finding anyone who would fit into her family any better than the guy by her side.

She pulled her attention from her noisy family and focused on the table across the aisle. Four young women, still dressed in their ski pants and sweaters, hovered over martini glasses rimmed with pink powder. They were laughing and pointing at a table of guys across the room.

Leigh Ann cut a generous bite off her steak, held it midair on her fork. "Joie and I decided to use Nils Ribi, a local photographer. He's unbelievably talented. Right, Joie?"

"Yeah, he's great." Over her shoulder, Joie could hear the girls laughing again.

"Speaking of photographs, I thought your future husband might enjoy seeing what he's getting." Leigh Ann smiled smugly, reached inside her bag, and pulled out an old deckle-edged photo. "This is what she looks like before hitting the bathroom in the morning."

Clint tentatively reached and took the photo, examined it. Immediately, he broke into laughter. "Oh, that's classic," he said.

Joie didn't have to look at the photograph to know what he was seeing. Leigh Ann had pulled this trick many times with plenty of boyfriends. The image was of her wearing one of her dad's oversized flannel shirts and a fuzzy pair of bottoms, part of a costume she'd worn in a school play—a bunny costume.

"Idaho gets cold in the winter," she said, defending herself.

"What's with the wild hair?" Clint asked, still chuckling.

"Oh, be quiet," she answered, grabbing for the photo. "I simply hadn't combed it yet." Pasting a smile, Joie reached for her knife and fork.

Someone tapped on her shoulder. She turned to find one of the girls from the neighboring table. "Are you Joie Abbott?" she asked.

Joie hesitated. The girl barely wore makeup, had long,

straight brown hair worn parted down the center, like Ali McGraw in the movie *Love Story*. She looked nice enough, but Joie couldn't quite place her.

"I saw you on the hill this morning," the girl offered. "I just wanted to tell you that jump you made—it was awesome!"

Joie swallowed, felt Clint's eyes upon her.

She gave the girl a weak smile. "Uh, thank you. I—well, I wasn't up there long. I mean—I needed some sunshine this morning and just made a quick run."

Looking a bit confused, the girl simply shrugged. "Well, you're good. Just wanted to tell you."

CLINT REACHED across the seat of his truck to adjust the volume on the radio, taking care not to topple a can of Dr Pepper resting in the drink holder. "You want to talk about it?" he asked.

"About?" she responded, cautiously.

Clint leaned back, tapped the steering wheel with his thumb. She could see his jaw twitch, knew he was considering his next words carefully.

"I'm sorry I didn't tell you," she blurted. She felt her own eyes widen, immediately felt the shame she'd often experienced as a child when she refused to come clean on some infraction, like the time she failed to shut the gate to the chicken coop, and the foxes got in and killed her sister's prize laying hen—the one Leigh Ann meant to show in her 4-H poultry club.

"Look," she said, feeling defensive. "I needed some time. To myself. No one seems to understand that everything is coming at me a thousand miles an hour. In less than six months, I became a mother and now I'm going to be a wife. I started a law practice and—well, all this wedding business." Her lip quivered as she fought back the emotion. "I needed some stinking time to myself!"

"Okay."

"Okay?" She scowled, looked over at Clint. "What does that mean?"

A smile nipped at the corners of his mouth. "Do you think I care if you go skiing? Why didn't you just tell me?"

Joie felt foolish. She didn't have an answer for that. Why hadn't she just told him? She stared at her feet. "I—I don't know."

Clint reached across the seat, grabbed her hand, and squeezed. "Let's get something straight. There's nothing you need to hide from me, Joie. Going forward, let's agree we can tell each other anything that is on our hearts. Deal?"

She sighed, feeling even more foolish than before. Of course, he was right. "Clint, I'm sorry. I know you're right. I don't want secrets between us."

He studied her for a moment, his dark eyes narrowing to seek out the place where she couldn't hide from him. She didn't know whether to blush or be annoyed. "I think you're scared," he told her.

"Scared? What have I got to be afraid of?"

Clint gave her a sideways look, and Joie couldn't help but admire the way his hair carelessly brushed the tops of his ears. He had always been the serious one. Soft-spoken and studious and so very smart. But even though he was quiet, Clint saw everything. He understood things that the others couldn't, simply because he took the time to observe. Joie had always admired him for it. And in the end, it was Clint's evaluation she feared the most. He could see through her with the slightest glance.

"I guess I'm just a little overwhelmed," she finally admitted.

Clint nodded tightly. Like there was something he didn't want to say, not out loud. "I know what you're feeling."

"Yeah?"

"Well, sure. This is a big deal, this getting married business. All the details make me feel a bit uptight myself."

Joie was surprised to hear that. "Really? Because you don't look as untethered as I feel."

He got quiet. She didn't push, simply waited, knowing he'd find the words he wanted to say.

Clint rubbed at the back of his neck, finally confessing, "I'm not one of those guys who enjoys being in the spotlight. And I'm obsessing over writing my vows." He released a heavy sigh. "There's so much I want to say, and I'm unsure how to publicly express just how much you mean to me, how desperately I want to make you happy."

Joie locked eyes with this man who loved her, knowing this was her chance. This was the perfect time to risk letting down her defenses, an opportunity to open her heart and share herself—all her doubts.

It wasn't that she didn't want to get married. She loved Clint and wanted to be his wife. But how could she explain she felt like she was completing her life's puzzle with different pieces than had originally come in the box? That, at times, she felt like she was on the outside watching a version of herself who was a stranger. The idea of that sometimes sent her into a panic.

She couldn't. The notion didn't even make sense.

Clint pulled into her driveway, came to a stop.

Before he could cut the engine, Joie reached for his hand. "Wait," she instructed, needing a high that would make everything else fade away.

She unbuckled her seatbelt, then reached for a section of her hair and pulled her hand down the strands, slowly. She leaned in his direction, lowered her voice. "Did you know I like cowboys? Not just any cowboys, but men who wear Nocona boots and Stetsons."

Clint's eyes sparkled with amusement. "I wear Noconas."

"Um-hum," she said, moving closer.

"And I've been known to wear a Stetson on occasion."

"Is that right?" Her hand unzipped his coat as she maneuvered across the seat of his truck and onto his lap. She fingered the buttons on his shirt, traced her finger up to his jawline. "And I believe I've heard you say you love me desperately."

Clint nodded, his voice barely audible over the music still playing on the radio. "I—I've said that."

In a quick move, and with surprising strength, she pinned his arm against the seat.

Before she could take hold of the other, he reached and nested his fingers in her hair, pulled her face to him.

They kissed, long and hard. His lips tasted minty, and slightly of the coconut crème pie he'd eaten at the restaurant.

The warmth of his arms thawed the chill in her bones as she pressed against him. She let the intensity running through her body erase her angst and hoped the same was keeping Clint from dwelling on the mixed messages she seemed to keep sending. She loved him—wanted to be his wife. That was the only message he needed to hear from her right now.

"I love you," she whispered against his ear.

Clint pulled back. He drew a deep, jagged breath, coughed —looked at her with intensity. "I love you too, hotshot. But we're in a pickup here. Perhaps we'd better—"

"Take it inside?" She grinned, ready to scramble off his lap.

He traced his finger across her cheek, longing evident in his eyes. "As tempting as that sounds, don't you have a babysitter waiting?"

Drat! He was right. She'd totally forgotten that the neighbor girl was inside. She sighed, moved back into her own seat in resignation. "I'm sorry," she told him. "Maybe after I walk her home?"

"I think we'd better pass." He looked at her then, like he wished he could change the situation. "It's really late. I agreed to meet the Baxters before daybreak. Given the predicted snowfall, they want to board that new mare before they leave for Seattle."

Joie knew what he said made perfect sense. They weren't kids. They had responsibilities. Gone were the days she could party all night and call in sick the next day. Still, she hadn't earned her reputation by choosing sensible options. "You sure?"

He grinned, took her chin in the palm of his hand. "By this time next week we'll be married. I look forward to showing you what married couples do—on our honeymoon."

Joie burst into laughter. She gave him a fake punch in the chest. "Well, listen up, cowboy! Your soon-to-be-wife is looking forward to you fulfilling that promise."

6

Karyn sat in her car outside the real estate office for almost an hour. Her coffee in the cup holder was cold. She was wasting gas because it was too frigid to turn the car off and sit for more than a few minutes without running the heat, but she still hadn't worked up the nerve to go inside and talk to Tessa McCreary.

She sat pondering her habit of showing up so early. She supposed it was her incessant need to make sure no one had to wait on her. She hated inconveniencing anyone. Zane would make fun of her for it. He would have challenged her belief that everyone else and their needs came before her own.

Putting herself first felt selfish, but the times she'd followed his lead and expanded her experience, she'd felt like she was living, not simply existing. She could hear Zane now, almost as if he were sitting next to her with a cup of coffee in his hand. *"Today. This is what you've got. What are you going to do with it?"*

She wanted to live grand, wake up each morning with excitement, embracing the idea that the world offered more opportunity than she could possibly grasp. Everything was waiting for her. She simply needed to take hold of it.

Karyn turned the key in the ignition, cutting the exhaust but leaving it in the position where the radio would still play. When she got too cold, she told herself, she'd go inside.

Less than ten minutes later, her chattering teeth told her it was time, and she did just that.

The minute she stepped through the door to the office, Tess drew her into a hug. "Karyn! Come in. Get warm!"

Karyn handed off her scarf and coat. Tess hung both up on a beautiful antique coat rack near the window.

"Thank you for agreeing to meet me," Karyn told her. "And for keeping all this confidential. I simply haven't made any permanent decision and—well, you understand."

"I do," Tess assured her. "Why don't you come on in my office and I'll show you some comps I pulled. I think you're going to be pleasantly surprised at the prices. Your house is going to sell at top dollar. The market is hotter than it's been in years."

Karyn raised her eyebrows. "Really? Even in the dead of winter?"

"Especially now. We're in the middle of the ski season, and there's few offerings on the market."

Karyn swallowed a lump building in her throat, wondering if she was making the right decision. This was the house she'd shared with Dean. She'd spent hours in those rooms mourning his loss, learning how to pick up and move on. She'd lingered more hours reeling from Grayson's decision to return to his ex-wife in order to raise his baby boy.

Every street, every shop held a memory. She and Grayson had their first date at the Ram, sat on the benches in front of the Opera House. That was where she learned he'd been married before, that he, too, had had his heart broken. The area in front of the pavilion was the site of Dean's memorial fundraiser. And that interminable Hemingway memorial, where she'd taken Dean's—

She felt her gut twist.

Exactly!

Those were the exact reasons why she needed to sell—why she needed to disentangle from the past and move on.

The short time she'd spent with Zane in California taught her there was still much happiness ahead. She didn't know how that would look, how it would all play out. Yes, making this kind of change felt scary, yet the idea of a potential new life was exhilarating as well.

Zane lived his life never spending more than a few months in any one place. While that may not be her ticket, certainly she could pull up roots—even if temporarily—and experience something new just this once.

What could possibly go wrong?

Her gut twisted again.

Instinctively, she knew what could go wrong. Her family would have a fit, especially Leigh Ann.

LEIGH ANN KNEW her sisters called her "The General" behind her back, but she didn't care. She didn't care because all of them knew what it was like to grow up without a mother, to know that there was no one to help you plan your wedding, no one to help you pick out the cake, or choose your wedding dress, or sit in the front row pew in tears as you walked the aisle.

Leigh Ann leaned forward in her bathroom mirror and applied her mascara, carefully so as not to smudge any black on her eyelid.

Joie may not think she wanted all these things, but Leigh Ann knew better. Every girl longed to have their special day shared with someone who had watched her grow up and thought she was the most beautiful bride ever. She would be that for Joie this week. Even if her younger sister didn't seem to want it.

And then there was Karyn. Poor, lost Karyn.

Her middle sister had experienced enough loss in the last couple of years to last a person a lifetime. Unlike Joie, Karyn was not tough. Her heart didn't mend so easily. When times were at their bleakest, her sister had even tried to self-medicate to alleviate the pain she'd felt after losing not one, but two men.

Had it not been for Mark and his financial tumble, she'd have bought a ticket and gotten on an airplane—headed to Alaska and given that Grayson Chandler a piece of her mind. The absolute nerve!

He'd scooped up a bird with broken wings and just when the tiny creature was healed enough to fly, he'd tossed it into the street to get run over. Admittedly, the analogy was a bit graphic, but the image perfectly depicted what Karyn had been through. She'd been run over, in more ways than one.

Goodness, how her sister had kept from falling apart at the seams, she didn't know.

She sighed, shoved the tiny black brush back into her mascara, and applied a second coat.

She hated to admit it, but the trip with Zane Keppner seemed to have done Karyn some good. She could see that. Her sister's face was brighter, her voice lighter and filled with hope. Even so, she was glad she was back home, where she belonged —where her family could care for her and love on her.

They were as different as night and day, she and her sisters, but they were linked forever, arm-in-arm. They'd seen each other through so much. She wasn't sure she'd have made it through Mark's financial upset, and what his partnership with Andrea DuPont had done to their reputation in this community, had it not been for her sisters.

She closed the lid on her mascara, examined her face in the mirror. Satisfied with her appearance, Leigh Ann turned and headed through her bedroom suite and into the hallway, smiling as she glanced at hanging photos of Colby when he was a baby, of him and his new wife.

Despite the fact her daughter-in-law had robbed her of planning her own son's wedding, Leigh Ann had determined it best to move past the hurt and was trying to be friends with Nicole, even withstanding how different as she was from the wife Leigh Ann had envisioned for Colby.

She'd grown to be thankful to have Nicole in the family, especially lately. Her daughter-in-law had been a huge help. Nicole agreed to assemble the votive candles—one hundred of them. Leigh Ann wanted to place them all around the lobby, add to the ambiance during the reception.

That was only one of many final details that needed attention over the coming days. For example, she needed to confirm the harpist would play six sets instead of four, as misstated in the contract she'd only received via email last evening. For the life of her, she couldn't understand why people waited until the last minute for everything. She'd had to prod far more than she cared to in order to get all the details wrapped up for this production—and it was a production! But, oh—she had missed putting on big events. Those pitiful rivals at the tourism council made a huge mistake in letting her go.

This wedding would be a celebration of grand scale that would not only illuminate Clint and Joie's love story but would show everyone in this community that indeed, Leigh Ann Blackburn was back!

7

J oie was eating alone at her desk when her law partner, Maddy Crane, rapped on the partially open door then popped her head inside. "Hey there, darlin'! You up for lunch?"

Joie's mind drifted to the package of peanut butter crackers she knew was inside her desk drawer. Privately, she indulged the idea of passing on the idea of going out to lunch so she could continue working on her motion for summary judgment, but only momentarily considered it. If Maddy asked her to fly to the moon, she'd pack her bags and head to the airport. By offering to start a law practice together, the woman had given Joie her dignity back, and she owed her everything.

"Sure." She closed the deposition transcript. "Where are we going?"

Maddy couldn't contain her smile. She motioned for her to follow. "You'll see."

People were often surprised to find Madeline Crane looked very little like the image most persons had of a strong-minded, successful woman attorney. Joie had never seen her in a classic business suit. Instead, she dressed like one of those ladies on the *Designing Women* show she'd seen on that vintage television channel. For example, today she was dressed in a flowing black skirt topped with a ruffled light pink blouse and stiletto heels decorated with tiny bows. Her overcoat was made of the finest white wool, trimmed in silver fox, and she wore matching gloves.

Margaret Adele scowled from her side of the receptionist desk. "You best be wearing some boots, Ms. Crane. You'll break your neck in those fancy things," she warned.

Maddy laughed and held up her large designer bag. "Don't you worry, sweet thing." She sat daintily on a chair near the door. "I've got the situation covered." She opened the bag and pulled out a highly fashionable pair of furry black boots. "See?"

"Good gawd," Margaret exclaimed. Her hand slammed against the cleft of her ample bosom. "Where in the world did you get those things?"

"Do you like them, Margaret Adele? I bought these boots in Switzerland while on a honeymoon with my third husband." Like any good Southerner, Maddy said *third* without pronouncing the letter R.

Margaret Adele huffed. "They look like small puppies!"

Maddy didn't stop laughing until they were in the parking lot.

Joie moved to the passenger door of Maddy's Mercedes Benz G-Class SUV, a vehicle her law partner had ordered after seeing a report that there was no better luxury car for driving in the snow. "So, do you think Margaret Adele is the right fit for our reception area? I mean, she's pretty gruff." She opened the door and slid inside. "I'm not advocating letting her go, of course. Perhaps we could move her into an accounting position, something more suitable to her personality."

Maddy climbed into the driver's seat, clearly amused. "Well, Margaret Adele is no oyster, I'll give you that. Yet, over the years, I've found women with the hardest shells, the ones who rub people like sand, often end up being the rare pearls. Margaret Adele has our backs." She grinned and started the engine. "Besides, sweet thing—it doesn't hurt to have people just a little scared of her, especially opposing counsel."

Joie couldn't help but smile. Maddy had a point. "I'd never thought of our receptionist as a secret weapon, but I can get onboard with that.

Maddy drove them to Enoteca, a quaint eatery only blocks from the office. They were seated within minutes. Maddy declined menus. Instead, she ordered a wood-fired pizza, rattling off the toppings from memory—sun-dried tomatoes, prosciutto ham, extra mozzarella cheese with arugula lettuce on top. "Perfect for a blustery day," she said.

She leaned forward in her chair and got right to the point, the reason she'd invited Joie to lunch. "I've got the prenuptial agreement for you." She reached in her bag and pulled out a folder, slid it across the table.

"Wow. That was fast." Joie took the folder, opened it.

"I think you'll find all the provisions are set forth just as you directed. Our partnership agreement addresses the division of assets in the event either of us is no longer a partner in the firm. I simply refer to our partnership agreement and recite incorporation as if set forth in its entirety. The standard language."

Joie nodded her approval. "Everything looks in order."

Maddy leaned back, fingered the silverware on the table. "So, when do you want to have Clint come in to sign?" She paused, watched Joie from across the table. "Why the look? Is there a problem, darlin'?"

Joie quickly slipped the papers back in the manila folder. "Okay, can I confess something?" She cringed as Maddy waited, looking like she knew exactly what was coming next. "I—I haven't discussed this with him yet."

Before Maddy could respond, Joie rushed to explain. "I meant to. Many times. And he won't have a problem with it. It's just that—well, I kept thinking I had plenty of time. Now the wedding is in a few days, and I'm finding all these details are snowballing. It all seems so silly when there's so much work to do on my cases."

"Is that why you went skiing the other day?"

Joie swallowed uncomfortably. "No—I, well—I just needed some time. To be me—you know, before everything changes."

"Look, sweet thing. I've been married four times, so perhaps I should refrain from doling out any advice, but I've learned a tad in the process of all those relationships. The details do matter. Oh, not how you might expect, darlin'. The fine points of the ceremony—the music, flower selections, table decorations—those will never even be remembered ten years from now. But—" She paused, looked over at Joie with a look so raw it took Joie by surprise. "There are moments—events that in a split-second change life forever, and before you know it—you're somewhere else. Marriage is one of those moments. Don't miss out on the important parts. The things that will matter in the future."

She took her glass of water and jiggled the ice against the sides. "One thing is certain—a divorce does not begin when one person looks at another and says, "I want to put an end to this." The divorce begins long before those words are uttered, and sometimes as early as before the vows are said. If you are not open and honest with your spouse about what you fear, the marriage is over before it starts. It begins when the hurt begins, when you come to the astonishing realization that you are lonely even though you are married, that you feel ineffably alone even though you are with the person that you vowed to be with all of your life." Her eyes grew shadowed. "And believe me, the divorce doesn't end when the papers are signed. Its life span is unpredictable and open-ended. Divorce is simply the process of institutionalizing that loneliness. No courtroom win diminishes that."

Maddy shrugged, blinked away the emotion from her eyes. She took a sip of water. "Anyway, sweet thing. Take it from me. If there's anything you're holding back—don't."

Joie considered what Maddy told her, knowing every word was true. It was the kindness in her partner's voice that broke her. She realized she wasn't judging her. She was only pointing out the situation for what it was.

Of course, she needed to be open with Clint. Trouble was, how could she possibly tell him what she feared most—that things were moving forward so fast, she could barely keep up. Despite so many positive changes in her life, inside she was still the girl who preferred the feel of the wind in her hair, the thrill of taking risks, and waking up to the unexpected.

Yes, she was a mother and would soon be a wife—but fundamentally, she was still Joie Abbott.

There was no hiding the fact that she'd always been a mess of sorts, but admittedly, she liked who she was. Oh, not the bad choices that had wrecked her life on so many levels, but at her core, she was feisty and smart and liked living big. She couldn't bear the thought of a tamer version of herself.

Did Clint even know that?

What if he woke up one day and realized he'd made a horrible mistake? There were times she couldn't believe he hadn't gotten cold feet already and called everything off.

Maddy studied Joie's face. "Oh, darlin', you look like you just hugged a rosebush. I didn't mean to—"

Joie shook her head. "You didn't. Everything you said was spot on. I'm going to talk to Clint—about everything," she promised, vowing inside to set things right. "Soon."

8

L eigh Ann made her way through the lobby of the Sun Valley Lodge wielding a clipboard loaded with check-off lists. With less than a week to go before the wedding, a significant amount of details needed juggling, more than even she could keep track of in her head.

Outside the massive windows, the scene was beautiful. Huge clumps of snow drifted slowly through a blanket of frosty air, accumulating on the pine trees, bending the limbs low.

The skating rink lights reflected off the crystals. It was true —snow could glisten.

The area was experiencing a near record year in terms of snow fall, and from the looks of things, the weather had no intention of letting up anytime soon. An outsider might fret over the predicted blizzard wondering if conditions might put a hamper on their ability to drive, but she'd lived in this area nearly her entire life. She, and everyone who lived in Sun Valley, certainly knew how to maneuver a few feet of fresh snow without crisis.

Leigh Ann stopped midway through the lobby to straighten

a large portrait of a fly fisherman casting a fuzzy nymph across Silver Creek. The painting was an oil on canvas rendition of a photograph by a local photographer named Nils Ribi.

She stopped, made a note to seat Nils and his wife next to Miss Trudy. As artists, they would have much in common, which would make for good table discussion.

She smiled to herself, feeling entirely in her element. She'd loved filling in for Karyn as hospitality director at the Sun Valley Lodge. But the job had always been temporary. Now that Karyn was home, she'd return to her position, and Leigh Ann would again be without a job. Not that she needed the money, Mark provided more than adequately. She got a lot of pleasure out of utilizing her abilities, and appreciated the accolades that always followed.

This wedding event was not only a family celebration, but an opportunity to put her skills on display once again. She'd suffered a lot of blows when her husband was wrongly suspected of cheating many of the townspeople during his partnership with Andrea DuPont—including the humiliating termination of her voluntary services for the tourism council. This was her chance to turn everything around, to make the council members reconsider and maybe even invite her back.

It would have to be their idea, of course. She'd imagined the scene in her head a thousand times, dreamed of what it would be like to receive an email asking if she might possibly be available for lunch. The meal would be catered, and there would be flowers on the conference table. They knew she loved flowers.

Sitting around the table was Betty Lionel, a CPA. Les Rickart and Marsden Winder owned one of the most successful property management outfits in town. The Dilworth sisters—Trudy and Ruby attended every meeting without exception. There were others, many she'd known for years, including Leo Gabbert, the Chamber of Commerce director.

She remembered the day they asked her to resign as if it

were yesterday. Never had she experienced such humiliation. She had every right to remain angry, to seek retribution. Instead, she was the sort who believed true requital was better accomplished by making them regret that decision.

Surely, they'd been impressed to learn she'd worked with Horace Mikel and coordinated his Vanguard Conference months back. Now, she was putting on the social event of the year! Each one of them wanted to be included, and she'd made sure hand-engraved, linen-printed invitations arrived in their mail-boxes. She would seat each council member strategically to be in full view of every wonderful detail—the deep golden hue of the Cristal champagne, the perfectly grilled filet of beef with garlic mashed potatoes and mushroom sauce. And not just any mushrooms, but morels plucked off the sloped sides above McCall.

For dessert, there would be a Sylvia Weinstock wedding cake, flown in from New York City at a cost that would make old Betty Lionel drop her dentures. The cake was a gift from her and Mark—extravagant, but worth every penny.

In no time, the council would be begging her to come back. Who else could orchestrate such grand events? And Sun Valley had their share of events—they needed her.

Across the lobby, a fire crackled in the massive rock fire-place, creating a cozy atmosphere, despite the twenty foot ceilings. The steady hum of the Zamboni resurface machine circling the ice rink mingled with instrumental music piped from carefully hidden speakers.

Leigh Ann hummed along as she made her way down the long hallway lined with framed vintage celebrity photographs and headed in the direction of the spa. She needed to confirm the appointment she'd arranged for her and her sisters. She was choosing the exact shade of polish for her toes from the rack on the wall—Pagoda Pink—when she heard her name called.

"Leigh Ann Blackburn?"

She turned to find an impeccably dressed woman walking in her direction. She wore dark gray wool slacks and a crisp button-down white shirt with a scarf tied around the turned-up collar. Her boots were Rag and Bone, crafted of camel-hued suede with lamb shearling trim. She'd seen the exact ones on the Barney's of New York website last week.

"Yes, may I help you?"

The woman extended her hand. "I've been stalking you." Her face broke into a warm smile as she shook Leigh Ann's hand. "In in a nice way."

Leigh Ann was instantly flattered. "Oh?"

"Yes," the woman said as she reached inside her pants pocket, pulled out a business card and handed it to Leigh Ann. "I'm Croslyn Merritt—editor of the Happenings blog."

Leigh Ann found it hard to swallow. "Happenings? Oh, my! I read that daily. Love it."

The woman grinned. "I'm glad. That makes my request so much easier."

Before Leigh Ann could respond, Ms. Merritt went on to explain. "I'm here in Sun Valley doing a story called *Forty-Eight Hours in Sun Valley*. The piece focuses on life in the resort town, its history, of course, but primarily I intend to shed light on how residents live among the celebrities that frequent the area. A "day in the life" composition, if you will."

Leigh Ann beamed. "That sounds wonderful." She tucked a strand of hair behind her ear and tried to act nonchalant. "What can I do to help?"

Ms. Merritt's gaze turned razor sharp. "I understand you are hosting a family wedding later this week here at the Sun Valley Lodge. I'd like to attend, take photographs, and incorporate the event into my article."

Leigh Ann was at a loss for words. She certainly hadn't expected *this*. "Well, of course! I mean, anything I can do to

raise awareness of our resort area and the Sun Valley Lodge."
She quickly tucked the business card in her pants pocket and
pulled out her cell phone. "Perhaps the easiest way to do this is
for me to give you my electronic contact information." She
scrolled through the addresses stored in her phone until she
landed on her own name, then she hit share.

Immediately, Ms. Merritt's phone dinged. She slid her
elegant finger across the face of her phone and accepted the
data exchange. "Perfect!" she said. "I'll be in touch soon."

"I look forward to it," Leigh Ann replied, nearly stammering
over the words.

Croslyn Merritt wiggled her fingers in a wave, turned and
headed for the elevator.

Leigh Ann stood there, absolutely stunned. A fine bead of
sweat sprouted on her forehead as she came to an astonishing
realization. Her entire world had just done the jitterbug on the
dancefloor of luck.

"Croslyn Merritt—editor of Happenings," she whispered
out loud, trying to take it all in, as she paced. This was the coup
d'état of a lifetime. In an instant, her scrappy existence had
been overthrown and she'd found herself hob knobbing with
one of the most respected women internet journalists of her
time.

With contacts like Croslyn Merritt, the world was
suddenly her oyster. Secretly, she'd imagined herself writing a
blog read by women everywhere. This might be the open door
to that dream coming true. She could parlay this situation
into a potential endorsement. This was only the start of what
could be ahead! And at no better time now that Karyn was
back and would return to her position at the Sun Valley
Lodge.

Even better, she wouldn't have to grovel in front of the
tourism council members. She could jump higher and faster—
leave that situation and her hurt feelings behind.

Leigh Ann quit pacing and put her hands on her hips, squeezed her eyes shut and willed herself to calm down.

She was a woman walking up to the door of middle age. Even so, she felt as lighthearted as a kid. If there weren't so many people mingling in the spa, she might have done a real live cartwheel!

9

"And you said yes?" Karyn pinched the bridge of her nose, unable to believe what had just come out of her sister's mouth. "Leigh Ann, you know Joie will have a fit."

"We don't know that. In fact, she's not wired the same as you and me. For example, just look at how she's pulled back from this entire wedding planning process. You and I sweated over each detail when we were planning our ceremonies. Would it be better for our bridesmaids to be lined up at the front according to height or how long we'd known them? How many chords of the wedding march should play before we tucked our arm in Dad's and marched down the aisle? Joie cares about none of that. What makes you believe she'll get in a huff over a few media people taking pictures at her wedding?"

"Because I know Joie, and because those photographs will be seen by thousands across America? Happenings is the most widely followed blog among women age twenty-five to sixty. Do you know how difficult it is to land a feature spot? Zane was featured, but only after his publicist knocked on those doors for two years!"

"All the more reason to never turn down this kind of opportunity," Leigh Ann reasoned. "Not only will the spotlight on Sun Valley be tremendous, in terms of economic impact, but think of what this could mean for me personally."

"You?" Karyn lifted her brows, moved her phone to the other ear.

"Yes, me. Have you stopped to wonder what I'm going to do next? We both know filling in for you here at the Sun Valley Lodge is only temporary. What if the tourism council digs in their heels and never invites me back? What then?"

Karyn realized with a start that her older sister was scared, afraid her days ahead might be filled with planting flowers and decorating and canning tomatoes. It broke her heart to understand that so much of Leigh Ann's worth was tied up in her vocation.

She hesitated. Was it time to share her plans?

As soon as the notion entered her thoughts, Karyn shut the idea down. It was entirely too soon. She didn't even know her plans entirely yet and was still vulnerable to pressure. This was a decision she must make free of coercion from family members. They meant well, but Karyn knew their support would be lacking, motivated by their love and concern for her, of course. Still, she was at a big crossroads, and this would have to be her decision. Besides, she wanted to do nothing that would detract from Joie's big day.

She'd tell Leigh Ann and the rest of her family soon—but not yet.

"Well, I still think you should get Joie's approval before committing," she told her older sister.

There was a pause on the other end of the line.

"You already committed, didn't you?"

"Yes," Leigh Ann admitted, then rushed to explain. "But trust me. Our little sister is not going to care, so long as there's no media circus. And Croslyn Merritt has assured me in a number of texts that they will do their business quietly and behind the scenes. They will be interviewing some guests but will be very nondescript in their approach."

Karyn knew Leigh Ann didn't believe all that she was saying, but she was desperate, and the argument served her purposes. "Well, I'm on the record disagreeing. But it's your cake to bake. Be careful not to burn it."

Karyn hurried to end the call, hung up the phone.

This was exactly the thing that wore on her spirit. She adored her sisters, but the family drama could be draining. She needed space to breathe—to start over and do life fresh and free of expectations and others' disappointments.

She had more emotional baggage than she could carry. She didn't need to drag other people's burdens along too.

Of course, she wasn't naïve enough to believe her sisters wouldn't be calling on a regular basis. They'd still be in each other's lives, but not in such close proximity. Living out of state would grant her the opportunity to create distance when needed, and keep her head on straight.

The close call with drug dependence had scared her enough to make some necessary changes. She must put herself and what she needed to be emotionally well first, for once.

With that resolution firm in her heart and mind, Karyn headed for her bedroom. She stopped in front of the bureau and tugged on the top drawer, sliding it out.

Inside, wrapped in a piece of satin that had been cut from her wedding veil was a box. She lifted it carefully, fingered the crossed skis engraved on the lid, then tucked the tiny container in her purse and headed for the door.

~

THE SCENE before Karyn looked very different than the last time she was here. The wild poppies and blue flax, pungent skunk cabbage poking up from the pebbled ground lining the trail—all was covered by several feet of snow. In the distance, she could see someone had trudged through the snow-covered path, made their way to the rocky streambed and the pile of flat stones with its stately column rising from the middle.

A dull ache spread across her chest as she zipped her parka and pulled her woolen scarf tighter. She reached across the seat and took the small wooden box in her hand and climbed from the vehicle.

Immediately, her breath turned visible in the frosty morning air. The sound of water pulled her toward the monument nested against a stand of aspen trees, now bare.

Karyn trudged forward, her boots sinking in the snow with each step, until she reached the water's edge. With her gloved hand, she swept the frozen accumulation of snow from a creekside bench and sat.

Water bubbling across a rocky streambed was all that interrupted the silence.

"Hey, Dean." Her voice echoed, caused a tiny snow bunting to take flight, leaving its shelter of pine boughs.

She closed her eyes, tried to settle her jumpy nerves. This had not been an easy place to visit—not since leaving Dean here all those months ago.

"It's me, Karyn." She let out a sigh. "I know it's been a while. I've been— Well, it's a long story." Ignoring the cold seeping through the layers of clothing and against her backside, she continued. "Let me start off by saying how much I miss you, Dean. There's not a morning I don't open my eyes and think about you. Not a day passes that I don't still wish things had been different."

Karyn gazed out across the snow-covered golf course beyond the trees. "I know you would want me to move on. And I tried. I really did, Dean. I even met someone right here at this very spot. His name was Grayson, and while our relationship did not end as I had hoped, he helped me realize I could love someone again, even while carrying you in my heart. For that, I will always be grateful."

She brushed the snow from the bench. "Still, I didn't weather the breakup well. I struggled, fell into a deep emotional pit and started using unhealthy methods to escape the pain. But those days are over. A new friend talked me into taking a risk and doing something completely out of character. You would have loved it, Dean. I climbed on the back of a motorcycle and took off down the open road." She couldn't help but smile. "I so wish you and I could have built memories like that before you left. You would have loved Glacier National Park. And man, no doubt you would've looked great in a pair of leathers."

Karyn let herself laugh out loud. "Knowing you, we would have pulled over often for a little doodle-bopping along the way."

She drew a deep breath, happy for the good memories, and turned her gaze to the sky. "I've made a big decision, Dean. I'm leaving. I listed the house this morning. My heart will always hold a piece of Sun Valley close, and my family and your parents remain my firm foundation. But I need this. I need to be *me* for a while. I know you get what I'm talking about."

The tops of the pines gently bent in the frigid breeze.

"One of the things I loved about you, Dean, was your free spirit. You never faltered, never feared pursuing your dreams, your passion, with everything you had. It didn't mean you did not love me when you took off for Olympic trials—sometimes for weeks on end. You believed your two highest loves were not in competition, that you could have both me and your skiing. That you could be everything you might become. You loved me well. I have no regrets."

She dropped her gaze to the snow at her feet. "I don't believe I will have any regrets about this decision either. I'll need your help, your spirit, to help me be strong. You know I will get a lot of pushback. I'll be made to feel selfish for taking care of *me* this time."

Dean's often spoken words rang in her memory. "Life is not a spectator sport, Karyn. Win, lose or draw, the game is in progress, whether we want it to be, or not. So, go ahead, argue with the refs, change the rules...cheat a little, take a break...and tend to your wounds. But play. Play hard. Play fast. Play loose and free. Play as if there's no tomorrow."

Karyn stood, planted her feet firmly in the snow. "I intend to, sweetheart. For you—and for me."

10

J oie stood at the bathroom mirror, staring at her reflection.

She hated bridal showers. If things had been left up to her, she would have skipped the entire scene. But of course, Leigh Ann would have none of it. "What? Miss your bridal shower? But what about all your friends? They want to celebrate with you. Besides, this is a rite of passage."

Joie had responded by dropping her gaze to little Hudson, nestled in her arms. "I think my rite of passage has sailed already."

Leigh Ann huffed, slipped a pan of lasagna into her fancy Thermadore oven. "Nonsense! Getting the horse before the carriage does not disqualify you from all the trappings that go with getting married. One day, you'll look back and be sorry you failed to embrace the celebration this event deserves."

Joie knew full well that when her oldest sister got some fire in her belly over something, she became unstoppable. Leigh Ann Blackburn could be a force of nature. She was better than anyone at making her case until you broke down and gave in to her. There were no teams in arguing with Leigh Ann. No buddies. You were on your own.

Joie spritzed some cologne and gave a final inspection in the mirror. Satisfied, she turned and headed into her living room where Clint was rocking Hudson while he watched *Wheel of Fortune,* his eyes squinted in concentration as he stared at the television.

"Brownies and Ice Cream," she said as she bent to kiss him goodbye.

"Huh?"

"The puzzle. It's 'Brownies and Ice Cream,'" she repeated, pointing.

He turned his attention to Vanna White and the puzzle. "That's amazing. How do you do that?"

Joie shrugged. "It's a gift." She turned and headed for the door. "Thanks for watching Hudson. I won't be late."

When she pulled up in front of Leigh Ann's, the number of cars parked up and down the street caused her heart to pound. She didn't even have that many friends, which meant the free rein she'd extended to her sister had turned into a full-blown rodeo.

Truth was, she'd just as soon head over to the stables and run Fresca around the arena a few times rather than spend several hours with Party Barbie and her gaggle of guests.

Too late now.

She zipped her parka tight and climbed from the car, made her way to her sister's front door, and rang the doorbell.

The door flew open, and Leigh Ann immediately ushered her inside. "Here she is. The guest of honor."

Her sister's hand went to her zipper as if she were a child who needed help. "Leigh Ann, I got it," Joie said in frustration.

Leigh Ann obliged and dropped her hands, then whispered in frustration, "Where have you been?"

Joie smiled at the crowd of women. "Sorry I'm a bit late,

everyone. I had to get Hudson down and then ended up behind a snow plow. You know how it is. Those things are impossible to get around."

Cindy Taylor stepped forward and pulled her into a tight hug. "Goodness, yes. It's really coming down out there. And we're supposed to get more later this week."

Joie hugged her back, surprised to see the owner of the stables. "I didn't know you and Dan were back in town."

Cindy raised the champagne glass she was holding. "Wouldn't miss any of this. Dan and I feel we played a small part in your big romance."

It was true. If the Taylors had not passed her over for the manager position and hired Clint instead, she might not be wearing an engagement ring on her finger. She'd been hot about their decision at the time, but how could she have known Maddy Crane would move to Sun Valley and offer her a partnership at the law practice? Life seemed to have a way of turning out the exact way it was supposed to.

As if on cue, Maddy waved from the back of the room, glass in hand and dressed in a stunning turquoise and shell pink ski sweater with turquoise leather pants. "Hey, darlin'."

Joie scanned the crowded room. The Dilworth sisters were there, of course, and Dee Dee Hamilton. No doubt, they'd brought the lovely floral bouquets that graced every table in Leigh Ann's house. Ariana, her sister's fitness instructor, looked chic in her size-two jeans. She gave a wave of greeting as their eyes met.

In the kitchen, her sister's housekeeper, Isla, was busy pulling trays of some sort of food from the oven. The savory aroma made her stomach growl.

Pam Curry and Julie Phillips linked arms and led her to a beautifully decorated table. "Look what your sister put together. Isn't it great?"

Joie nodded. Her sister had definitely outdone herself. The

scene looked like a page taken straight out of some bridal magazine.

Pink material draped a long table with a four-tiered cake in the center. Near the end of the table, a delicate arch of white balloons with tiny pink roses and greenery tucked inside was mounted on a panel of rustic wood with hand-lettered scripted words spelling out *Bride-to-Be*. She'd seen one similar on a Hallmark movie she'd watched with Karyn some months back.

Piles of beautifully wrapped packages were stacked all around, making it nearly impossible to stand in front of the table. Another smaller table was filled with champagne bottles and a punch bowl with floating scoops of some sort of frozen concoction. To the right of the champagne, crystal flutes were lined up perfectly next to silver trays filled with homemade mints.

"Your sister always goes all out," Julie said. "I've never known anyone who could bang out a party better than Leigh Ann."

"Yeah, she's a real velvet hammer," Joie muttered, feeling a bit out of place. The shower decorations were lovely. Obviously, Leigh Ann had gone to a lot of work. But the truth was, she never enjoyed being the center of attention at things like this.

Her sister clapped her hands together. "Attention, everyone. Now that our guest-of-honor has finally arrived let's get this party started."

As soon as everyone was seated, Leigh Ann motioned for Karyn to help her and they passed out little sheets of paper and pens. "Okay," she said, beaming. "This first game is a series of questions to see how well we all know the bride-to-be and her intended."

Joie had to fight to keep from rolling her eyes. Only Leigh Ann would use a word like *intended*. Even so, she forced a smile and took a pen.

Isla beamed as she made her way around the guests and filled their glasses with bubbly.

"Okay, first question," Leigh Ann announced. "In Clint and Joie's relationship, who made the first move? Simply mark bride or groom on your paper."

Several of the guests quickly marked their answers. Others paused, grinned back and forth at one another before marking their papers.

"That one's easy," Miss Trudy announced. "Clint had to get up in court and announce to the world that he was in love with her before she'd see it."

Joie cringed. That wasn't true!

Well, maybe...a little.

"Okay, next." Leigh Ann puffed up like a marshmallow, and her voice turned as saccharin. "Here's a great question. Who is messier? Bride or groom?"

Karyn giggled. "This one isn't even fair." She took a long sip of her champagne.

Paula swept her long blonde hair off her shoulder. "Dang, girl. You can't argue this one. In high school, you'd open your locker and never fail, junk would tumble onto the floor in the hallway."

"That's not true," Joie argued, feeling a little picked on.

Ann was quick to join in. "And the backseat of your car held more clothes than your closet at home, if I remember correctly."

Joie grabbed the bottle of champagne from Isla's tray and topped off her glass. "You people all have poor memories. And if you're not careful, I'll be looking for some replacement bridesmaids."

That remark seemed to make everyone laugh. A good thing, she supposed. She found none of this very funny.

Finally, the game ended. Cake was served, and Joie began to

hope the party was close to winding down even though it'd only just started.

"Okay, it's time to open the gifts." Leigh Ann motioned for Karyn to help her, and they moved to the piles of pretty wrapped boxes and gift bags with bows located near the cake table.

A lump of frosting caught in Joie's throat. "Here? Now? But I thought that happened later."

Miss Trudy popped up off the sofa. "Oh, no. We all get to watch you open your shower gifts. That's half the fun." She handed off a package wrapped in paper with little red hearts. "Here, open this one first!"

Joie smiled, but it wasn't her happy grin. She obliged, carefully unfastened the taped ends and pulled the wrapping paper back. Inside was some carefully folded yellow material. She lifted the garment to find a risqué nighty with little motorized silver stars fastened at the breasts that spun and flashed tiny lights. She immediately flushed red. "Oh, my!"

Miss Trudy threw her head back and laughed. "Wipe the look off your face, Joie, dear. It's a gag gift." She turned to her sister, Ruby. "Isn't it, sister?"

Ruby, piped up. "Well, that naughty thing certainly makes me gag."

Everyone in the room laughed, many of whom Joie didn't know well. She hadn't stacked up a lot of girlfriends since high school. Most of her friends were men—her skydive buddies and the guys down at Crusty's, who played pool and watched sports on television. Except for her sisters and Maddy, she didn't have a lot in common with the female persuasion.

For the next half hour, she tore printed paper and opened boxes, peeked inside, then ooh'd and ah'd over the contents. There was the obligatory crock-pot, cookie sheets and one of those air fryers she'd heard about while waiting in the grocery line.

"You'll love it," another of her friends from high school claimed. Joie couldn't remember the girl's married name but thought her first name was Jan and she lived somewhere in Utah now. "My Dirk eats fried chicken as if he were Colonel Sanders. He jumped up two sizes in his jeans before I pulled the plug and told him, '"No, sir. No more fatty foods for you.' But with my new air fryer, he can eat all he wants." She turned to Dee Dee Hamilton. "Chicken is healthy if you don't load it with Crisco."

Joie stared at the bubbles in her flute. The girl reminded her of a television commercial. Even so, she had to hand it to her. At least she could cook.

Cooking didn't come easily to her. She had to really concentrate on the recipe, talk out loud to make sure she was measuring correctly, and it was impossible for her to chat on the phone at the same time, like both her sisters could so easily do.

She couldn't imagine racing home from a hearing to cook a chicken. Thankfully, Hudson was still completely happy with milk. Still, there was no denying that she was on the brink of having to think about domesticity and how that might impact her life.

Karyn returned after helping Isla open more bottles of champagne. She plopped herself on the floor next to Joie, grabbed a homemade cheese puff, and popped it in her mouth. "What's the matter, sis? You look like you just sucked a pickle."

After what seemed like hours, Leigh Ann handed her yet another beautifully wrapped box—a rather large one and the last one left unopened. "Here, this is from Karyn and me."

Inside was a set of cookware—an obviously expensive set consisting of eight-inch and ten-inch fry pans, two-quart and four-quart covered saucepans, a covered sauté pan, and a large stockpot.

She lifted out the small saucepan. "Wow, these are—uh, really nice."

Leigh Ann beamed. "They're All-Clad polished stainless steel. The same set I have. They heat slowly and evenly, are oven and broiler safe and have a lifetime warranty."

Karyn gave her shoulder a brief hug. "I voted for a set of crystal, but Leigh Ann told me it'd likely end up donated to the Gold Mine Thrift Store."

She stood. She'd had enough smiling over gifts that she was supposed to want, many she didn't even know how to use.

She knew she couldn't stay the same and had to change. What kind of wife would she be otherwise? But, was she *this*?

"Thank you, everyone," she said. "I've had a lovely time, and I appreciate everyone and all this." She motioned with her arms. "The party was amazing, but it's getting really late—well, and I need to get home."

She may as well have been a pin pricking their party balloon. The mood in the room instantly deflated.

Paula and Ann exchanged glances before Paula quickly stood from where she sat on the sofa. "Yes, it's getting late. I still need to hem my little girl's dress, the one she'll wear to the wedding. I thought she'd be able to wear her Easter dress, but she's outgrown it. We bought her another, but she's between sizes, it seems."

Ann jumped up as well. "Yes, I have an electrician coming in the morning." She looked over at Leigh Ann, who sat stunned. "Can we help clean up?"

Her sister insisted she had everything handled. She hugged all the guests as they were leaving, thanked them for coming—as did Joie. Karyn busied herself helping Isla, often glancing over at the door with a worried look on her face.

As soon as Leigh Ann bid the last guest goodbye and closed the door, she whirled to face Joie, fuming. "What was that?" she nearly shouted. "You didn't have to act so rudely!"

Joie watched her sister scoop up some dirty utensils and stomp to the dishwasher in the kitchen, cram them into the little basket inside. She swallowed. "I wasn't rude."

"You were rude," Leigh Ann argued, her back to Joie. "Tell her Karyn. She was rude."

Karyn slipped onto a barstool at the counter, shrugged. "Well, I wouldn't call it rude exactly. I mean, she just said she had to get up early, and—"

"Oh, c'mon." Leigh Ann turned to face them. She rolled her eyes. "Quit covering for her. She was rude." Without waiting for a reply, she turned to Joie. "These people were here tonight to honor you and your upcoming nuptials. Is this how the wedding is going to go as well? Because if this is how the ceremony is going to go down, I'm out now. I'll have no part of it."

Joie almost wished she could take Leigh Ann up on her offer, even if made simply out of anger. "I wasn't trying to be rude," she said, defending herself. "It's just that—" She paused, not able to find the words to explain how the walls had been closing in, how she could barely breathe. She sighed, knowing from past experience she'd never be able to convey anything to her sister when she was in a huff. "Look, I'm sorry. I didn't mean to spoil the party."

"Sorry doesn't cut it!" Leigh Ann slammed the dishwasher door closed with her hip. "I don't understand you, Joie. Really, I don't. You're acting like you don't even want to get married."

Joie's heart pounded in her throat. "I do want to marry Clint. I just don't enjoy all—*this*."

Karyn swung back and forth on the stool at the counter, scooped a dollop of cream cheese frosting from a slice of cake lying untouched on a plate. "Then why are you doing all this? Why not just run off to Reno and say your vows in one of those little wedding chapels?" She licked her finger.

Joie stared at her like she had two heads. "Really? Do you remember when you and Dean initially thought you'd get married in Vermont while Dean was in trials at Stowe Mountain?" She pointed in their sister's direction. "She came unglued."

Leigh Ann's eyes instantly filled with tears. "Well, kick me for wanting to be at my sister's wedding."

Joie instantly felt like a heel. "I didn't mean—"

Leigh Ann held up her hands. "No, no. I get it. I'm the mean older sister who forces you both to comply with my wishes, regardless of what you want. I forced you to get good grades, pushed you into college, made sure you both had bathroom drawers filled with make-up after—"

"—after Mom died," both Karyn and Joie said in unison.

Leigh Ann stomped her foot. "Okay, that's enough Leigh Ann bashing for today!" She grabbed an open champagne bottle, poured the remaining contents into a coffee mug. "I refuse to sit and let the two of you point fingers and claim I made your lives hell. I didn't. Neither of you has a clue what it was like—"

"—managing the entire household at age sixteen," they again finished for her, this time laughing.

Joie lifted the mug from Leigh Ann's hand. She slipped her arm around her big sister's shoulders. "I get it." She looked around at all the wrapping paper on the living room floor, the gifts piled on the sofa. "You worked hard to make tonight special. I crapped all over it." She looked her sister in the eyes. "And I'm sorry."

Karyn joined them, enfolded her arms around the two and hugged her sisters tightly.

Together, they all made their way to the sofa. Karyn dug in the bowl on the coffee table and pulled out a handful of nuts. "Joie, something's definitely up with you. Why don't you just tell us what's going on?"

Joie looked at the mug in her hand. "I would if I knew." There, she'd described the situation as clearly as she knew how.

Of course, her answer shed very little light on why she was acting the way she was, why she always felt like she was simply acting like a version of herself.

She lifted the mug, took a long drink.

"I think I know how you're feeling," Karyn offered. "When life shifts, you have to sidestep a little to find your footing."

Leigh Ann pulled her hair back and wrapped it into a messy bun. She looked at the two of them, disconcerted. "I don't get it. She's getting married. She should be happy."

Joie tilted her head, considering how to answer. Deciding nothing she could say would help her sister to clue in, she instead locked gazes with Karyn. "It's—it's complicated."

Leigh Ann had had enough. She stood. "At some point, every person needs to make a decision to be happy. Self-imposed boundaries simply fence you in. Life is messy. That's how we're made. So, you can waste your life drawing lines and asking no one to dare cross them—but be careful. You may run out of time to create that life you two so desire." She placed her hands on her hips. "If you ask me, you both just need to get over yourselves."

She turned and headed in the direction of the kitchen. "Now, get up, you two," she called back over her shoulder. "I need some help cleaning up."

ON THE WAY HOME, Joie thought long and hard about the evening, the faux pas she'd committed in ending the party early. Why didn't she feel more onboard with these wedding rituals? Other women adored the showers, the cake tastings, the fittings. Why not her?

The mess inside her head was so distressing, she pulled her car off the road and parked outside Crusty's, a local bar located in a historic red brick building on Main Street. The bar, her former hangout, was named for the owner with a no sunshine attitude but a heart made of pure gold.

"Beers all around," Joie called out, slapping her credit card on the well-worn counter. "Except for me. I'm going with a club soda and lime."

"You got it. You all ready for the big day?" The balding proprietor with shoulder length gray hair pulled three pitchers from a shelf behind where he stood.

She shrugged. "Yeah, getting there."

Crusty smiled back at her. "Yeah, I hear you." He positioned the glass containers beneath a tap, tilting each until a perfect inch of foam covered the amber liquid, then slid the pitchers down the counter with precision to his waiting patrons. Next, he pulled frosted mugs from a small refrigerator next to the cash register and clunked them down. "So, we haven't seen you in a while."

She moved onto a stool. "Been really busy. The law practice, the baby, now all this wedding stuff."

Crusty pushed Joie's credit card back at her. "Your money's no good today."

She shook her head. "Thanks, Crusty, but you've got to quit giving all the beer away."

Grinning, he loaded a tall glass with ice, filled it with club soda and squeezed a lime wedge over the top. He plopped the glass down in front of her. "Eh, I'm doing all right in that department." He winked.

Joie nodded. "Gotcha." She lifted the glass in a toast. "Go high or go home." She smiled before tossing her head back and draining the cold carbonated drink. Finished, she planted the glass back on the counter.

"So, we're all excited for your big day," hollered Phil from at the end of the bar. "I even bought a new suitcoat for the occasion."

Terrance Cameron, her friend who used to teach African

American Studies at Berkeley, nodded from the barstool beside her. "Yes, the event of the year, I hear."

Joie turned forlorn. "Yeah, if I don't mess it all up." She told them about the bridal shower and all that had been on her mind. "I'm not sure I'm made out for all this domestic business."

Terrance rubbed his sparse beard. "Yes, a dilemma. Yet, I'm uncertain you're looking at the situation from the proper perspective. Take, for example, the women of Zulu. The bride changes into a traditional Zulu outfit. During this ceremony, the family of the groom slaughters a cow to show that they are accepting the bride into their home. The bride puts money inside the stomach of the cow while the crowd looks on."

Joie turned up her nose. "Not sure how that fits here."

A tiny smile sprouted on Terrance's face. "The suggestion here is that customs vary—and all these ceremonial wedding rituals are nothing more than outward signs of the commitment you are making. Don't make them bigger than they are."

Crusty wiped his hands on his bar towel. "Well, but she has a point. Sure, the ceremony is one day out of what is supposed to be a lifetime. But a man does have certain expectations of his bride—beyond the obvious."

Joie swirled the ice in her empty glass. "Like?"

Phil moved closer, beer in hand. "Like what she said. Clint will want a meal on his table on a regular basis. She's going to have a hard time if she doesn't know how to cook."

"I know how to cook—" Joie exchanged glances with her bar buddies. "Just not very well."

Crusty extracted her empty glass from her hand, turned to fill it up. "That's no problem. You simply follow a recipe." He turned, placed her drink on the counter in front of her. "If you can trace precedence and draft a legal brief, then surely you can measure ingredients and cook 'em up."

Terrance agreed. "I hear there's a new social media that is all the rage. Pinterest."

Joie's brows lifted, amused. "How do you know about Pinterest?"

Terrance straightened his jacket lapel. "I like to think I'm well-read—and keep up on such things. Social mores are my thing, you know."

She nodded. "Well, you may be right." Joie loved how these men got her. It's why they were her friends, and perhaps why she had trouble connecting with women who always over-thought everything and filled every situation with unnecessary drama.

She thanked them, hugging each before she headed back out to her car. While dark, the streetlights cast enough bright-ness to make out the snow-draped buildings down Main Street.

She breathed in the crisp night air and let her mind drift back to the day of the Dean Macadam Memorial, how she'd been late for the event and got in trouble with her sisters because she'd stopped by Crusty's for a quick beer. It was there she first laid eyes on a cowboy with a bear tattoo and a way of seeing through her crap.

He'd challenged her to a game of pool, in which she soundly beat him. She'd fully intended to continue her shame-less flirting until she remembered her family obligation.

It wasn't until later she learned he'd been hired as the new stable manager, a position she'd been vying for. Humiliation immediately formed as she realized his first impression would not be professional, but of her bending over the pool table in tight jeans.

Joie climbed into her car and looked out the window. It had begun to snow again. Big, huge clumps of flakes. In the distance, the accumulation weighed down the pine tree limbs, laying them low. Much like she felt.

She didn't deserve Clint. He'd been so good to her. Never

judged her—not even when she'd foolishly walked back into a relationship destined to burn her. Not when she became pregnant. Not when she had to fight Andrew for custody.

He'd been by her side through it all, never wavering in his support.

He loved her.

The idea of that truth startled her to the core, even now. More sobering—she loved him.

Never before had she been able to make that claim. There'd been guys, lots of them. Most, except for Andrew, were casual relationships meant to pass the time—hopefully with a shot of tequila in hand, followed by a beer chaser.

Andrew had been her *step over the line*—her dangerous foray into a relationship that was safe because it was forbidden. She didn't need a shrink to unravel that one. Married men were ultimately unavailable.

But this—this relationship with Clint both thrilled her and at the same time, scared her to death. This kind of love was not safe.

Joie lowered her car window. Frigid air hit her face as a slight breeze caught the limbs of nearby trees, sending snow swirling to the ground. She drew a wet and cleansing deep breath, relishing the ache the cold air created in her lungs.

She'd never been in love before. Not like this.

Now the tears came, rare tears.

She lacked the words to adequately describe him. It was as if she needed another language to explain how he made her feel—a language she wasn't sure she was ready to learn.

But learn it she would. He deserved the best—her best.

She'd go to dress fittings, she'd write her vows, she'd walk an aisle on her daddy's arm in front of tons of people watching —because she owed that to him, and more. She'd do whatever it took for him never to feel sorry he loved her, to never regret the fact he'd asked her to be his wife.

Headlights reflected in her rearview mirror, broke through the darkness. Joie quickly raised her window, blasted up the heater and moved to put her Jeep in gear. Unfortunately, the bright lights turned into red flashing lights.

She sighed and pulled her hand back and waited, realizing it had begun to snow fairly hard now.

A tiny rap pulled her attention to the window. Outside the glass, she recognized Rory Sparks.

She quickly lowered the window. "Hey, Rory."

"Joie? What're you doing out here?" He looked at her face, grew concerned. "You okay?"

Her hand quickly wiped across her face. "Yeah, yeah—I'm good. I just needed some air to clear my head."

He shook his head, confused. "Well, you best head on home. Just got a report over the radio from the National Weather Service out of Boise. Looks like we've got a big storm on the way." Before she could respond, he motioned with his flashlight. "I'll follow you just to be safe."

"That's not necessary, Rory. Really, you don't need to bother."

From the look on his face, he was having none of it. "Safety of our residents is my job. It's no bother at all." He tipped the rim of his hat and walked back to his car.

The drive home was more treacherous than she expected. Visibility was poor in the driving snow. She hated to admit it, but knowing Rory was right behind her did provide a lot of security.

Minutes later, she pulled into her driveway. The lights were still on in the house. A glance at the dashboard clock told her she was more than an hour later than when she'd told Clint she'd be home. She should've called him so he wouldn't worry. She'd have to get better about those kinds of things.

Joie cut the engine, grabbed her purse and climbed out of

the Jeep. She gave a quick wave in the direction of Rory's police car. He flashed his headlights, then slowly pulled away.

On the porch, she stomped her boots to knock off the snow onto the large mat just outside her front door. She inserted her key into the lock then opened the door to find Clint asleep in the rocking chair. Hudson was on his chest, also sound asleep.

The scene warmed her heart and made her smile.

Joie tossed her purse on the sofa, then gently lifted her tiny son from Clint. Neither of them woke.

After tucking Hudson into his crib, Joie returned to the living room, knelt in front of where Clint sat. She lightly touched his face, the rough growth of beard that appeared even though he shaved daily. His dark, copper-colored eyes opened slowly. The look he gave her was so raw, it caught her by surprise—the way his gaze caused the isolation she'd felt for years to fade.

"Hey," he said, his face drawing into a slow smile.

"Sorry I'm late."

He sat up, rubbed his eyes. "Did you have fun, babe?"

"I—I'm not sure." She knew her answer was confusing, at best. "But I fully intend to going forward."

11

The next day, Joie had a few minutes of free time between client meetings. She fixed herself some ramen noodles in the breakroom microwave and took them back to her office to eat.

While waiting for the noodles to cool, she parked in front of her desktop and typed *PINTEREST* in the search bar. She'd heard of it, of course, but had never ventured to check out the social media platform.

After setting up an account, Joie pecked around a bit until she landed on some photos of food—dishes that looked far better than her bowl of noodles. She clicked around and landed on a profile page with hundreds of recipes pinned. "This is exactly what I need," she said out loud and with great enthusiasm, despite the fact no one was there to hear her.

There were recipes for chicken dishes, for pasta, for low-carb main dishes, and wonderful desserts—all with photographs to show how they were supposed to look when finished. Her culinary skills were frankly limited to warming up take-out. But this—well, this could take her cooking ability to a whole new level!

Terrance was right. She could easily follow these recipes and cook like a pro.

She pulled a tablet of paper from her desk drawer and a pen, then thought better and scooped her phone off her desk and dictated the ingredient lists into her note app. When finished, she grinned.

She had a plan.

Today was her last day at work before the big day. Maddy had made sure of that. So, as soon as the last client left for the day and she'd finished with everything on her desk that had to be done, she scooped up her bag and headed out.

Margaret Adele looked up from the receptionist desk. "Sorry, I couldn't make the bridal shower last night, kiddo. It was Bunco night down at the Grange Hall. My night to bring prizes. You understand."

Joie nodded. "Of course. No worries."

"I'll be at that wedding though. I'm not usually one for dressing up for all that church stuff, but the cake always makes attending worth it," she said tightly, then paused. "Just don't expect me to do any dancing, or anything. I hate all that."

Joie smiled weakly. "I'm glad you're coming."

Outside, she stood at her car wondering if Margaret Adele was married. It had never dawned on her to find out or to learn if she had children. You weren't supposed to ask those things in a job interview, and she'd never been that interested in the details of her employee's life before now. That, too, should change. She wanted to be a nicer person—someone who wasn't only focused on herself.

Admittedly, all these upcoming transitions were terrifying, but she might as well jump in to her new adventure with both feet. This was her chance to be a better version of herself, a more loyal sister and friend, a great wife and wonderful mother. She intended to embrace the idea of change, would temper her natural bent to just wing it, and get on with this new life.

With that pledge in mind, Joie left her car and crossed the parking lot on foot heading in the direction of Atkinson's Market, taking care to follow the shoveled pathway. Inside, she made a beeline to the meat counter with the same focus she often used when preparing a motion for summary judgment.

Marley wiped his hands on his apron. "Well, hey. How's the future bride?"

Joie took a breath, smiled. "Great. I'm here for some boneless cut pork chops."

Marley moved to the glass display and slid open the door, pointed at some neatly stacked chops. "Got these in fresh this morning."

"Great!" She pulled out her phone, checked her notes. "I'll take a pound."

Minutes later, he handed her a tightly wrapped package. She tossed it into her cart. "Thanks, Marley."

"You're welcome. See you at the wedding!"

"Yup. See you there." Joie placed another smile on her face, bid him goodbye, and moved for the produce department.

With phone recipe in hand, she bought baby bella mushrooms, shallots and cloves of garlic, then scoured the aisles until she located a box of organic chicken broth. It took a little longer to find the marsala wine and all the spices she needed. Finally, she had her cart loaded with all the ingredients she wanted. She headed for the check-out counter, only diverting momentarily to pick up a bottle of Ste. Chappelle cabernet from the wine aisle.

"There she is. The beautiful bride-to-be!"

Joie looked up to find Elda Vaughn standing in the line in front of her. The woman clasped her dimpled hands together enthusiastically. "I was so delighted to get the invitation in the mail. I adore weddings!"

Joie looked at the woman she'd known for almost her entire life. "Hey there, Elda. So glad you plan on attending and helping us celebrate."

The woman unloaded the contents of her cart onto the moving conveyor. "Will your dad be there? I mean, of course he'll be there. What was I thinking?" She giggled nervously.

Elda Vaughn was one of the Bo-Peeps—the women in town who had a crush on her father. The ones who tried to win his favors with baked goods and homemade treats.

An amused smile nipped at the corners of Joie's mouth. "Yes, Dad will be walking me down the aisle during the ceremony."

Elda's face immediately lit up. "Of course! The whole thing sounds so romantic. I hear from Dee Dee Hamilton there will be lots of roses. And the Dilworth sisters say your dress is being flown in all the way from California." She batted her eyes in an exaggerated manner. "How magical! It really is true—love reigns."

Joie could smell her heavy perfume. She often wondered what drove some people to use too much fragrance. Surely their minds told them three sprays were enough, but it's as if their brains said, "What the heck, I'll just go with thirteen."

Before Joie could politely extricate herself from the conversation, Elda cleared her throat. She glanced both directions so as not to be overheard. "I—I bought my own wedding gown. On sale back in 1989. It's hanging in my back closet in a bag. Unfortunately, I never found the right guy." Her expression brightened. "But I have my eyes on someone."

Joie didn't dare follow-up on that loaded statement. "Well, I'm glad you can come to the wedding."

Inside her bag, her phone buzzed. Joie pulled it up, glanced at the face. "Sorry, I need to get this." She turned and slid her finger across the screen. "Hey, Leigh Ann. What's up?"

"Your final fitting. Can you stop by after work?"

"I'm already off work. I stopped by the grocery store to pick up a few things. I plan on making dinner for Clint."

"Oh?" Leigh Ann's voice suddenly turned all sing-song—the same voice she used when talking to donors at charity events. "What are you making?"

"I found a recipe on Pinterest for pork marsala."

She could hear her sister nearly choke. "You were on Pinterest?"

Joie lifted her chin. "Yes, I was on Pinterest. Why?"

She waved goodbye to Elda and unloaded her items onto the conveyor.

There was a slight pause on the other end of the phone. "Well, you strike me more as an Instagram girl, that's why."

Joie held back her annoyance—barely. "If you must know, I'm on Instagram, Facebook, Twitter, LinkedIn, Snapchat, and now Pinterest."

"Okay, okay. I was just saying . . . " Leigh Ann's voice drifted off. "Well, never mind."

Remembering her resolution to get on board with all the wedding trappings and to be a nicer person, Joie pulled her debit card from her wallet. "So, what time do you want to do the fitting?"

Another pause came, then Leigh Ann responded, sounding a tad cautious, "Well, why don't you stop over first thing in the morning? I'll have the coffee on and some pastries."

"That sounds great, Leigh Ann. I'll be there first thing in the morning." She slid her card into the reader, punched the required buttons.

She was about to tell her sister goodbye when Leigh Ann inserted one more thing. "Joie? Pork marsala is a very compli-cated dish. Maybe you should try something a bit easier—perhaps spaghetti?"

Joie swallowed her irritation, took a deep breath. "Thanks, but I think I'm good."

Another pause. "Well, if you run into any problems with that recipe—call me. Okay?"

~

JOIE PULLED a shallow pan from the cupboard and scooped some flour into it, added the salt, pepper, and garlic powder and stirred the dry ingredients with a fork.

She wasn't sure what all the fuss was about. The guys were right. Reading and following a recipe was a lot like checking citations in a brief. Even a starting paralegal could do the task, providing he or she had access to a good set of Westlaw books, or better yet, the online app.

She poured herself a glass of wine, then carefully unwrapped the pork chops. After checking the recipe for the next step, she dredged a chop through the flour mixture, sending a little cloud into the air. As the recipe directed, she repeated the process until all the chops were dusty white.

On the stove, oil was heating in one of her new pans. She carried the plate of chops over and added the meat to the shallots and mushrooms already browning. The immediate sizzling sound startled her, and she jumped back to avoid the splattering grease, vowing to choose a dish less messy next time.

Ha—and her sister thought she was incapable of following a simple recipe. With satisfaction, she pulled her phone up again—checked the instructions.

Lower the heat and let simmer for 10 minutes.

Okay, done. She covered the pan with a lid and returned to the counter to mince the thyme leaves. After adding the herbs to the simmering mixture, she busied herself with cleaning up.

After loading the last dirty utensil into the dishwasher, she picked up her phone, blasted off a test to Clint.

I have dinner cooking. Don't be late.

Seconds later, her phone dinged, signaling an incoming text.

Dinner? Sounds great. Love ya!

From down the hall, Hudson started crying. Joie quickly wiped her hands on a kitchen towel and headed that way.

"Hey, sweetheart. What's the matter?" She picked up her son, kissed the top of his downy head. He sniffled, buried his face against her chest.

Her hand patted his bottom. "Oh, my goodness, little one. You're soaked."

She hummed a little tune as she placed him on the changing table. The minute she removed the wet diaper, he kicked his dimpled legs.

"Yeah, that feels better, huh?" She reached for a diaper and some wipes. After cleaning his little bottom, she lifted and positioned him over the new diaper and fastened it, then snapped his little onesie back into place.

She sniffed, wondering why the air felt so heavy. It took several seconds for reality to register, before awareness flashed into her puzzled mind.

Smoke!

Fear gripped her.

She stared at the door in confusion, her feet stuck to the floor. "Move!" she told herself. She rapidly glanced between the door and Hudson's crib. She didn't dare leave her tiny son behind.

Her stomach turned rock hard, and beads of sweat burst onto her brow as she raced for the kitchen with him in her arms. On the stove, smoke billowed from the pan. She raced and grabbed for the lid, burning her hand. "Ouch!"

The lid clanged onto the floor. Thick brown smoke rolled upward from the pan and slithered like a fat snake across the ceiling.

She swore and quickly stepped back, shielding Hudson .

Flames suddenly shot up from the pan as the grease caught fire.

In a panic, she raced to the sink, cradling the baby against her hip. She grabbed a nearby glass, moved to the sink, turned on the faucet and filled it with water. Taking several steps toward the stove, she tossed the contents in the direction of the flames, taking care to remain what she hoped was a safe distance.

Sparks flew in every direction. Joie ducked, protecting her son with her body as a shield.

One of the bright red sparks landed on the nearby curtains. Smoke smoldered for a split second before the sheer fabric caught fire.

Joie held back a scream, eyed the towel on the counter. Could she use it to beat out the flames?

Before her mind could form an answer, the curtains burst into flames, blackening the surrounding wall.

Shaking uncontrollably, she realized this battle could not be won. In tears, she grabbed her phone from the counter by the sink and raced for the door.

Outside, she fought shaking fingers and punched out 9-1-1.

A voice immediately came on the line.

"I—I have a fire. Please help!"

12

Joie watched with utter defeat as two firefighters exited her house, rolling up a thick, black hose. One of them paused as they neared, his frame silhouetted against the lights from the fire engine. He removed his hat and tucked it under his arm. "The fire is out. Let's get you inside the fire engine with your son where it's warm."

Distracted, she realized she'd been standing out in the snow without a coat, and that she was indeed freezing. Even so, she shook her head, "No, that's okay. I'm fine."

He nodded but retrieved a blanket made of shiny silver fabric from the fire engine and wrapped it around her shoulders. "It's cold out. You don't need to get hypothermia."

"Can I call someone?" the second firefighter asked. Joie recognized his face but couldn't place him. She could barely think, let alone form any cognizant conclusions.

Before she could refuse his offer, Clint's black Ford Ranger pickup turned the corner in the distance and raced toward them.

He pulled into the driveway and braked hard, causing the pickup to slide in the snow. Before the vehicle came to a complete stop, the driver door flew open, and Clint poured out.

"Joie? Are you all right?" he shouted, as he raced for her.

Joie nodded. "Yeah, I'm good. My kitchen? Not so much." As his gaze met hers, she felt the familiar rush of adrenaline. He'd always had the ability to unsettle her, to make her feel off-balance, dizzy, her heart beating too fast, her words getting choked in her throat.

He grabbed her into his arms. "Oh, babe."

She tucked her head against his chest, stared at the familiar bear tattoo on his forearm, felt his strength—his protection. Her emotions rose like a wave. Her knees buckled, and she folded full into him. He scooped up the weight of her, pulled her tight. "Sshh—it's okay. I'm here now."

Like a baby, she sobbed. "I—I didn't mean to—I mean, I could have—my son."

Clint stroked her hair. "I know, I know. Everything's okay now. You're safe. Hudson's safe. It's going to be all right."

Out of the corner of her eye, she spotted her sisters climbing from Leigh Ann's car. "Joie! What happened?" Leigh Ann shouted as she raced forward.

"Are you all right?" Karyn asked, rushing to her side. "Where's Hudson?"

Joie pointed to the fire engine. "They've got him inside, staying warm."

Karyn nodded, patted her arm. "I'll go check on him."

Leigh Ann seemed to sense it wasn't time to grill her younger sister but couldn't contain herself. "What happened? How did the fire start? Is there much damage?"

Joie mentally dodged the questions being fired at her. Instead, she looked at Clint for strength.

"A pan on the stove caught fire. The damage is minimal, but could have been much worse," Clint explained.

Leigh Ann grabbed Joie's wrapped hand. "You got burned?"

She nodded. "I stupidly grabbed the hot lid without protection."

Leigh Ann shook her head. "Sounds like you were lucky."

"I don't know how lucky burning down my kitchen was," Joie told her.

"You know what I mean. Joie, what were you thinking?"

Joie clenched. Here it came—the judgment. "If you think I did this on purpose—"

"I'll go take a look, but everything can be fixed," Clint said, intercepting the exchange.

One of the firemen, the one who had been the first to arrive on the scene earlier, stepped forward. "We'll be finished up soon and you can go inside to survey the damage." He nodded in Clint's direction. "The damage was limited to one wall of the kitchen. Looks like two cupboards were destroyed and will need to be replaced. And you have significant smoke damage. I don't recommend you spending the night inside. But we often see much worse. You were indeed fortunate the damage was limited."

Clint shook his hand, thanked him. "I appreciate all that you guys did."

"No problem," the fireman said.

Karyn exited the fire engine with little Hudson wrapped in a blanket. "You guys can stay with me tonight."

Before Joie could respond, Leigh Ann piped up. "It'd make much more sense for you to come to my house. We have the fitting in the morning, anyway."

Joie turned to her sisters. "Yeah, it makes sense to go to Leigh Ann's, I suppose." She looked at Karyn, still feeling shaky. "But would you mind staying over too?"

Karyn nodded. "Of course. And we should probably call Dad before he hears about this from someone else." She handed off Hudson to Leigh Ann, slipped her phone out of her jeans pocket and stepped aside to place the call.

Sadness tightened Joie's chest as she looked at Clint. "Well, shall we go take a look?"

His arm went around her shoulders and squeezed. "Yup. Let's do it."

Joie told Karyn and Leigh Ann she'd have Clint drop her off later, asked if they would take Hudson, feed him, and get him to bed.

"Of course," they both assured her.

She kissed her tiny son's forehead, tucked the blanket tightly around him. "Mommy will see you soon, big boy."

Clint returned to his truck and brought a coat for her and a spotlight. Together they trudged up the snowy steps to the condo Joie had purchased nearly a year ago.

"Careful," Clint warned. "The floors are wet."

Joie grabbed his hand, followed him across the living room floor.

He stopped, held up his arm to keep her from proceeding. "Wait here."

She ignored him, pecked her way into the kitchen as he shined the light around. Her breath caught as she saw what she'd done to her kitchen.

There was black everywhere, heavy dark sooty black. Broken dishes littered the floor, as well as burnt pieces of wood. The knobs on the stove were melted, the glass on the digital microwave windows shattered. A strong odor of acrid smoke filled the air.

Joie couldn't help it. She teared up again. "Well, I really did it this time."

Clint didn't answer. He directed the light up to the ceiling. The surface was as black as the night outside. "Okay, we're not going to be able to do any real assessment until morning. Let's get out of here."

He saw her then. His face softened.

She'd allowed herself to hope, and now this. With the

exception of the law practice, it seemed everything she set her hand to was at risk. She'd stupidly followed her father up the mountain while eight months pregnant and had ended up giving birth to her precious son while leaned against a craggy rock, putting him in danger even before he took his first breath.

Today, she'd started their home on fire. She couldn't even think about all the possibilities—of what might have happened.

Clint reached and brushed a damp strand of hair off her cheek. "I know what you're thinking."

His words did little to douse the fiery ache inside her tired soul. All she'd wanted was to cook him a nice dinner. Those girls at the shower all seemed to be able to pull off the maga-zine-cover woman thing. They looked gorgeous in their designer jeans and tops, their rose-tinted hair with brunette tips, their powder nails in just the right shade of blush. They were so put together, such perfect wives and mothers. Always having everyone else's best interests at heart.

She was a mess! A mess that could draft a dang good cross-complaint, but a woman who could do little to resemble what most men wanted in a wife.

"Are you sure you want to go through with marrying the likes of me?" she asked Clint, gazing into his kind eyes. "There's still time to change your mind."

The comment made him laugh.

Suddenly, he turned dead serious. He cupped her chin. "You listen to me, Joie Abbott. I chose you. I believe you were meant to be mine since the beginning of time. You were created perfectly—and I am a fortunate man to be gifted with loving you."

His words were a salve, a balm to an open wound that never seemed to heal.

"I love you," she told him.

She moved close, nested her face against his neck, inhaling the familiar scent of him, all woodsy and musky.

Joie had never considered herself the kind of woman who yearned for a knight in shining armor, but just now the notion was appealing.

She felt the warmth of him through his T-shirt. Joie turned her face into his hand and pressed a kiss against his calloused palm. He was a man's man, a hard worker. Loyal to the death. So many good things. She wanted all of them.

She kissed the curve of his jaw, feeling the coarseness of his stubble against her lips and relishing him for the man he was.

His breath caught, and it emboldened her. With a hand against his face, she turned Clint toward her. Their lips met gently, and Joie soaked up his response. Her fingers tightened on the cotton material of the shirt.

Clint pulled her closer, into the strength of his embrace. His stomach was hard against hers, his shoulders like solid rock. He was a sure and steady foundation.

"Joie," he whispered.

The sound of her name on his lips, so desperate and devoted, was sweet and heady.

She wanted him.

No, she needed him.

He deepened the kiss, and Joie responded in kind, drawing her fingers through his collar-length brown hair, latching onto the wonderful thought that by this time next week, Clint would be her husband.

Forever.

With the thought came complete surrender. She ran her hands across the plane of his back and returned his kiss with an intensity that surprised her.

So, this is what real love is, she thought. It turns you from doubt and distrust, from betrayal and feeling like a failure—instead making you feel infinite and safe, like the whole world is open to you, anything is achievable, and each day filled with wonder. Maybe it's the act of opening yourself up, letting someone else in—trusting. Or maybe it's the act of caring so deeply about another person that your heart expands.

His love was a gift. She'd done nothing to earn it. There was nothing she could do—no mistake, no failure—nothing could diminish the love he had for her.

One thing she now knew for sure—if Clint was for her, who could be against her? And that changed everything.

13

J oie woke to bright sunshine streaming through the bedroom window, the first clear day Sun Valley had experienced in weeks of winter. Surprising, given the dire weather forecasts.

She threw the covers back and popped up, a strange feeling of joy bringing a smile to her face. She stretched her arms high in the air. It was going to be a great day!

No doubt she had overslept. After last night's drama, her body probably needed the extra rest.

She sat for several seconds, taking in the stillness, the only sound disturbing the silence the hum of a distant vacuum cleaner.

A sound outside the door finally broke her pleasant reverie.

"Joie? You awake?" The door slowly opened, and Leigh Ann peeked her head in. "I have coffee and some breakfast."

"I'm up. Come on in."

Leigh Ann juggled a bed tray filled with pastries, crisp bacon, scrambled eggs, and steaming hot coffee—black. Just the way she liked it.

"Wow, Leigh Ann. Thank you!" Joie exclaimed. "I'm famished."

"Well, eat up. The designer will be here with your gown in about an hour. I can't wait to see how you look." Her sister placed the tray on the bedside table. "Oh, and Daddy called. He's over at your house with Clint. He says you should just pack up and stay in your old room out at the ranch, then move directly into your new house after the wedding. It's only a couple of days. Besides, that will leave you free from the repairs that have to be made to the house here in town. Once renovated, Mark thinks you can market the property and make a tidy sum."

Joie shuddered at the memory of the blackened walls, the burnt cupboards. She tentatively slid a piece of bacon in her mouth. "That makes sense, I guess."

Leigh Ann scowled. "You shouldn't talk with your mouth full."

"Yes, Mother," Joie teased. She swallowed and grabbed for a pastry topped with cream cheese and some kind of berry filling.

Her sister rolled her eyes, waved her off. "You're impossible. Look, I've got a lot to do before the designer gets here. As do you, so eat up. Karyn will be here in about twenty minutes with Hudson. She took him with her when she went to pick up a few items at Atkinson's Market. Clint is going to help out and pick up the candles from Dee Dee. The legs of lamb have been delivered, and the kitchen staff at the lodge are doing all the prep work for the big rehearsal dinner. So far, everything is running smoothly and as planned." With a satisfied look on her face, she turned and exited, shutting the door behind her and leaving Joie to enjoy her breakfast.

The designer's name, she learned, was Julia DePontia. She flew in from San Francisco with a dress she'd designed from scratch using measurements sent to her by Leigh Ann. The gown was outrageously expensive, another wedding gift from Mark and Leigh Ann. A gift Joie had unsuccessfully tried to decline.

When she arrived, Julia was impeccably dressed and wore a faint but distinctive scent Joie recognized from the perfume counter at Dillard's. She looked amazing in alligator riding boots and tight jeans, with her long black hair pulled back in a ponytail, all of which made her look very young, as well as very chic. Standing next to her, Joie felt uncomfortable in an old faded Boise State sweatshirt, jeans with holes in them, and sneakers, but Julia gazed upon her warmly and didn't seem to notice what she wore.

She couldn't say the same for Leigh Ann, who gave her *the look* the minute she saw Joie's outfit choice.

"I couldn't wait to meet you," Julia said after they were introduced. "Leigh Ann says such wonderful things about you."

Ignoring Leigh Ann's sour look, Joie extended her hand. "Thank you for coming all this way."

They chatted for a few minutes. Joie learned Julia and her new husband had considered buying a vacation home in Sun Valley but elected to build in the Hamptons instead. She also learned Julia used seasons as verbs. "We summer there every year with my parents, and winter in the Bay Area."

Julia was quiet for a moment, then clasped her hands together. "Well, shall we get started?"

The gown was stunning—a gorgeous full-length simple A-line gown made of satin with a bateau neckline and three-quarter lace sleeves. The dress made her feel like a queen and was exactly what she would have chosen.

"It's beautiful," Joie whispered, breathless. "Really beautiful."

Leigh Ann beamed. "I knew that style would suit you."

Julia pulled a tape measure and some pins from her brief-case. "Let's make sure the fit is just right." She measured several places before reporting the dress would only require minor adjustments under the arms. "We're nearly dead on with our measurements." She turned to Leigh Ann. "You did a great job."

Her older sister inhaled the compliment and puffed with pride. "I'd hoped so." She turned to Joie. "You can wear Mom's white fox over-the-shoulder stole while outside. And I thought your long hair might look good styled in a messy upsweep with tiny cream buds tucked in the folds."

Joie gave her a warm smile. "Sounds perfect."

Leigh Ann was obviously pleased, and no doubt surprised at the lack of typical blow-back she received from her youngest sister. Joie rarely went along with her suggestions without a trace of complaint.

"No, I mean it," Joie told her. "Everything is absolutely perfect. Thank you." She moved and gave her sister a tight hug.

Leigh Ann tried to hide the emotion in her eyes. "I—it's my pleasure."

Julia folded the tape measure carefully and put it back in her bag. "Well, let's help you out of that dress, and I'll have it at the church in plenty of time."

Before she could start to get undressed, the door opened, and Karyn walked in with little Hudson all dressed in his blue snowsuit and fuzzy cap.

She stopped mid-step. "Oh, Joie! You look stunning in that dress."

Julia stepped behind Joie and carefully unfastened the back of the gown. "The promotional discount was extremely fortunate. Especially given the initial budget you proposed. We were able to do so much more."

"Promotional discount?" Joie asked, her eyebrows pulled into a frown. "What do you mean?"

Julia's ponytail swung wildly as she bent to straighten the gown's hem to help ease Joie out of the dress. "I'm able to substantially reduce the price given the dress will be featured in Happenings. I've tried to nail something down with Croslyn Merritt for over a year. This is a real triumph. I will be eternally grateful, Leigh Ann."

Joie whipped her head around. "What?

Her sisters exchanged worried glances. Hudson sensed the tension and started to fuss.

Joie marched over and took him from Karyn's arms. "Spill, Leigh Ann. What is she talking about?"

"We're extremely fortunate," Leigh Ann carefully explained, donning her most convincing tone of voice. "I was approached by the editor of one of the largest and most applauded women's blogs that is broadcast to literally hundreds of thousands of avid followers. She asked to feature this wedding." She pasted the widest smile possible. "Of course, I said yes. You don't say no to Croslyn Merritt. She's read *everywhere*."

Julia nodded. "You simply can't pay for that kind of endorsement. It's a real coup to land such a feature."

Joie didn't know about that. She did know her special day was not going to be turned into an advertisement for jewel-encrusted trophy-wife wanna-be's.

She shook her head vehemently. "Absolutely not!"

She caught the *I-told-you-so* look on Karyn's face, and continued, "This can't come as a surprise, Leigh Ann. I let you run with this. You've done a superb job with all these details. Much better than I could have done, for certain. But this? This is off the table." She turned to Julia. "The dress is lovely, but I'm afraid if full-price is not within budget. We'll have to pass. That's all."

Julia's mouth dropped. She spluttered, "I—I don't understand."

Leigh Ann, in an attempt to salvage the situation, took Julia's elbow. "No—don't worry. We'll purchase the dress at whatever price. And, the other—" She looked over at Joie.

"Well, we'll let you know."

Julia's ponytail hung perfectly still as the young designer tried to digest the sudden turn of events. "Well, sure—I guess I'll wait to hear from you then." She carefully packaged up the dress. "We'll get those slight alterations made and have the dress delivered to the church hours before the wedding." She lifted her chin, summoning her professional demeanor—held out her hand to Joie. "It's been a pleasure designing this gown for you. You are going to make an exquisite bride," she said tightly.

Joie thanked her and followed as Leigh Ann walked her out. As soon as the door shut, Leigh Ann whirled. "What was that? How could you simply say no without taking time to consider the matter?"

Joie's shoulders stiffened. "I could pose the same questions to you."

Karyn rushed over, stood between them as a buffer. "Let's not have a blow-up. We can talk about this."

Leigh Ann ignored her pleas. "Do you have any idea what you are turning down? Being featured on Happenings is akin to an entertainer being asked to host *Saturday Night Live*."

Joie brushed aside her sister's comments. "And I care that my wedding is paraded in front of a bunch of thirty-somethings who don't have anything more on their minds than their fifty-dollar blow-outs, Pilates lessons, and how much kale to put in their green juice in the mornings? None of that matters to me, and you know it. This was for you."

Karyn ran her hand through her hair. "Let's sit down and talk this out."

Stepping past her, Leigh Ann wedged closer to Joie. "So, what if it was? Is that so bad? Why would you care if Croslyn Merritt takes a few pictures and writes up something nice about your wedding celebration? You don't have to read it. In fact, if the matter hadn't come up today, you might never have even known." Her voice was now raised. "That's how much this would have made a difference to your special day."

Hudson started crying. Karyn lifted him from Joie's arms and quieted him by humming. Her phone dinged from on the coffee table.

Leigh Ann threw up her hands in surrender, still giving Joie a dirty look. "I'll get it, Karyn. You have your hands full."

Her fingers reached for her sister's phone. She drew it up, glanced at the screen for several seconds. Her expression darkened. She raised her gaze slowly, stared at Karyn with a deep frown.

"Why is a realtor listing your house?"

14

"You're moving?" Leigh Ann could barely breathe.

First Joie's fit over some inconsequential advertising promotion, and now this? Were her sisters turning absolutely mad?

Karyn's face filled with guilt. "I was going to tell you."

"When?" Leigh Ann demanded, not bothering to hide her anger.

"Yeah," Joie chimed in. "You're moving? When did your family get to know about this major decision? When the real estate sign went up in the yard?"

Leigh Ann couldn't help it. Her eyes filled with tears. "You can't move—I mean, we're a family."

Karyn looked at her patiently, yet with building sadness. "Just because I'll be living in California doesn't mean we're no longer a family. That notion is plain silly."

"In California? But that's miles away," Joie pointed out, taking Hudson from Karyn's arms.

"That's what they make planes for," Karyn countered. "It's not like I'll never see you guys. You're overreacting a bit, don't

you think? I traveled all the time with Dean when he was quali-
fying for the Olympics. This isn't so different."

Leigh Ann's lip quivered. "You won't live here. That's not a
little two-week jaunt out of the country, or a month-long vacation in California with some photographer you met—a road
trip filled with adventure. This is permanent. You won't be here
with us."

"You won't see Hudson grow up." While Joie rarely became
rattled, her lip slightly quivered. She turned away, dabbed at
her baby boy's lips with the end of a cloth diaper to hide her
disappointment. "He needs you," she quietly added.

It was clear Joie was clinging to any argument now. Leigh
Ann mentally applauded the effort, shored up the strategy with
her own line of reasoning. "Do you really want to live hundreds
of miles away from Dad—as he ages?"

The remark was playing dirty. They all knew it.

Karyn pled her case. "I'm not saying it's forever. Besides, like I
told you, there are airplanes. It's not like I won't still spend a significant amount of time here in Sun Valley." She crossed her arms over
her chest. "I'm not sure I can make you understand, but I've got to
do this." She paused, looked at them with a stubbornness Leigh
Ann had never seen in her sister's eyes. "I need this—for me."

Leigh Ann laughed bitterly. "We all need breaks from real
life, Karyn. We all have dreams we'd like to follow. But, some of
us aren't selfish. We realize that family comes first."

For a split second she felt a stinging regret, a sense that
maybe she'd said too much. Even so, she couldn't bring herself
to retract a single word.

Karyn looked at the floor, took a deep breath and then
gazed back up at her sisters. She seemed surprised—maybe
even hurt. Even so, something inside her seemed to build. She
laughed, deflecting. "Well, since we're talking about dreams,
let's discuss how you seem to always try to live yours through

me and Joie—and even your son. That is, if you're willing to look at the truth."

"What do you mean?" Leigh Ann challenged, her eyes signaling instant anger.

"I mean—take this wedding for example. You won't even hear what Joie is trying to tell you. You never had the big ceremony, instead had a quiet wedding without any fanfare, so you are taking over Joie's. On top of that, you didn't get to plan a big to-do for Colby when he married Nicole. We heard about that for weeks. I often wonder if you realize why he chose to keep you out of the picture until after the fact?"

Karyn may as well have slapped her. Leigh Ann looked between her sisters, trembling. "Is that what you two really believe?"

Their silence provided a clear answer.

She shook her head. "Did it ever occur to either of you to consider the sacrifices I made for this family—for both of you?" She looked at Joie. "Maybe I wanted to go to law school." She flipped her attention to Karyn. She took a step forward, pulled her blouse down off her shoulder, revealing her seal tattoo. "Perhaps I wanted some adventure, but this is about as daring as I allowed myself to go. I had a dark, handsome guy who clearly was enamored with me—his name was Thor. Did I stomp on my family to chase after him? Did I let my marriage go in the toilet, crush my son to give in to my little 'adventure?' No! I did not!" She didn't highlight how near she'd come. That wasn't the point.

She was nearly shouting now. She air-stabbed her finger at Karyn. "Since you think it's time to talk truth, let's explore why you're running? Did it ever occur to you that your problems don't stem from location, but from some deep fear that you're not good enough? You lost your footing, so you tried to escape with pills, and that didn't turn out so well. Now you are escaping by moving away. Face it, Karyn. A permanent change of scenery isn't going to fix what's broken."

"I'm afraid?" Karyn nearly sputtered. "What about you? You're so afraid the people you love will fail to live up to your expectations, you've placed a chokehold on all of us. Your love strangles us at times."

Joie tried to quiet Hudson, who was now fussing loudly. "Stop! You're both saying things you don't mean, things you can't take back." The look on her face was not convincing. She knew her sisters meant every word. Still, she reached for Leigh Ann's arm. "C'mon. I mean it. Stop."

In tears, Leigh Ann angrily yanked back her arm. She got quiet, paused, knowing she shouldn't say it, that there were some lines you shouldn't cross. But she was so tired of being judged, of being criticized and unappreciated. She couldn't seem to stop herself.

She looked at her sisters—so angry, so hurt—like she couldn't believe it. She couldn't believe they thought so little of her.

"Get out of my house," she ordered. "Both of you. Get out."

With fists tightly clenched, she turned and walked away.

15

K aryn's hands shook uncontrollably as she started her car. It was just like Leigh Ann to make this move to California all about her.

Everything about this was so maddening!

How could anyone fault her for waiting until after the wedding to share her news? What was she supposed to do? Ruin Joie's big day?

Of course, Leigh Ann had not thrown her fit because of the timing, but more likely because Karyn had the nerve to do something for herself without consulting her first.

This was exactly the reaction she'd been trying to avoid. Accusing her of being selfish and not caring about her family's feelings was completely out-of-line. Nothing warranted Leigh Ann's reaction—or excused how awful she'd acted.

Even so, the look in her sister's eyes as she kicked her own sisters out of her house would haunt Karyn forever. She never imagined her sister would turn on her, say those horrid things, make those accusations.

She was certainly *not* inconsiderate of her family—selfish

even! And she was not relocating because of some deep hidden fear.

Karyn gripped the steering wheel tightly, pulled away from the curb. Leigh Ann was sadly mistaken if she thought Karyn would allow such an attack, an imputation of her character, to go unchallenged.

For years, she'd done everything they all expected. After Dean's death, there were days she found herself puddled on the floor, unable to see any reason to get up. Leigh Ann marched her nosy self into her house without invitation, using a key she'd demanded days after she and Dean had closed on the house. "*In case of emergencies,*" she'd claimed.

No matter how bruised her emotions were, Leigh Ann demanded she get up and get dressed. Eventually, she'd even pushed her into counseling.

Of course, that course of action appeared so regal, especially when the Queen Sister was doing the urging. "*It's only for your good,*" she'd said.

Karyn stomped on the gas, pulling away from the curb and barreled down the street. She raised her chin. "I had every right to stay a mess for as long as I needed to," she said out loud. "Leigh Ann had no idea what I was going through. She's never been a widow and known that kind of grief."

And her older sister didn't know what it was like to suffer a second blow, what pain filled her soul when Grayson left her. Had her sister known there were times she fought wanting to not wake up?

Leigh Ann should be happy she'd rallied, had picked herself up and was embracing the future. Even if that future included living in California.

You don't drown by falling in the water. You drown by staying there.

A flicker of guilt crossed Karyn's mind. She'd said some

ugly things in return. No matter how truthful, she'd never wielded an emotional knife, cut someone she loved. And she did love Leigh Ann.

Much as she'd like to lay the entire blame at her sister's feet, no doubt she'd contributed to the fallout. She didn't know. Maybe she should have been honest up front.

Frankly, everything moved so fast after her appointment with Tessa, there was barely time. And she didn't want to do anything that might mar Joie's special day.

"Oh, I understand your reluctance to move forward with all this until after Joie's wedding," Tess had told her that day in the realtor's office. "But leave everything to me. We can quietly get your house appraised and listed. We'll not publicly market your house until you're ready. In fact, it's such a hot property, it's likely your home will sell without putting the listing up on the service. I get calls every day from people looking to buy."

That approach sounded reasonable, so Karyn signed the listing papers and put the situation out of her mind—at least temporarily. The way she saw things, it would take days for the valuation and a price to be determined, which would provide plenty of time for the wedding. She'd sit her family down soon after and explain. Of course, she knew they wouldn't like the news, but she would help them understand how happy she'd been in California, how much she was looking forward to starting a restaurant. With Zane's guidance and connections, she couldn't fail.

For the first time in a long while, she was excited about what the future might hold. Her family would see that and get onboard.

But then that text from Tessa.

She never expected this kind of blowback—was totally taken off guard by the intensity of Leigh Ann's anger. Her sister had gotten mean, even.

Without hesitation, she'd turned as abrasive. What did her sister think would happen?

She wasn't some lesser planet in Leigh Ann's orbit!

It had felt good to stand up for herself. But what was she supposed to do now? She couldn't remember a time when she'd been estranged from either of her sisters, let alone at war with one of them.

She and Joie would mend their differences, she knew. If anyone should understand the need for independence and a fresh start, it would be Joie.

But she wasn't so sure about Leigh Ann.

Despite her deserved stoicism, a dull ache formed in her heart. She feared there might never be a way to fix this—to turn back the clock. You can't unsay ugly things.

She swallowed hard and focused on the road.

Outside, the sky had turned dark, steely gray. Any moment it would start to snow again, adding to the snowbanks alongside the road. You could smell it in the air. The frozen scene left her feeling lonely.

Her phone buzzed from inside her bag as she braked at the stop sign.

Karyn pulled her attention from the naked winter trees outside her windshield, fumbled for her phone, and lifted it to read another incoming text message from her realtor.

Good news! We have an offer.

JOIE SLOWLY DROVE down the snow-packed lane leading to her father's ranch. Stands of bare aspens and willows lined the frozen banks of the east fork of the Big Wood, the meadow grasses, wildflowers now gone. Only an occasional sagebrush broke through the snow at the fence line.

A large hand-carved wooden sign that read *ABBOTT RANCH* loomed ahead in the distance. Beyond that were buildings, all made of rough-hewn logs—the cookhouse, the barn, and the bunkhouse, the riding arena and the small guesthouse where Joie used to live. Up the canyon, she could see the lambing sheds and the corrals in the distance.

The main house was on the left, an inviting log structure with an expansive lawn surrounding the building and a wraparound porch complete with a railing and rocking chairs. Tall windows lined both the front and back providing an unobstructed view of the stunning mountainous landscape dotted with pine stands. A river rock fireplace jutted from the southern end. Nearby, a woodshed filled to the brim promised warm fires to come.

Her father stood on the front porch. She waved, then switched off the engine and climbed from her car. She bent and greeted her dad's border collie with a pat on the head. "Hey, Riley. How are you, girl?" The dog's tail wagged wildly in response.

Her dad ambled across the yard. "Sweetheart, can I give you a hand?"

She pushed the passenger door open and retrieved her son from his car seat in the back, taking care not to wake him. She handed off her baby son into her father's large, calloused hands, enjoying his smile as peeked inside the blanket.

"How's my big boy?" he asked. He nodded in the direction of the newly constructed house built in the meadow to the right. "Clint's inside. Head on over and I'll take the baby." Without waiting for a response, he nestled the bundle next to his chest and headed for his front porch.

The air was frosty, the temperature dropping by the minute. Overhead, the sky had darkened with the threat of snow, as had been predicted all week. She headed for the front door of the home she'd soon move into—with Clint. That is, if she didn't burn that down too. It seemed a lot of things were going up in flames these days.

Clint looked up when she entered. "Hey, babe."

"Well, the wedding's off," she told him as she marched down the hall to what would soon become Hudson's nursery.

"What do you mean?" Clint asked, following her.

She laid Hudson's bag in the crib Clint had built. "Just what I said. We're eloping."

Clint turned the hammer slowly in his hand and grinned. "Is that so?"

"Yes. It doesn't matter that I now have the most beautiful wedding gown ever made, or that I look absolutely smoking hot in it—we're packing jeans and sweatshirts and heading to Vegas. I mean it. Get your suitcase."

Clint pulled her into his arms and kissed her. She let herself melt against him. When she put her arms around him, she found she couldn't let go. She held on so tightly he had to actually pull her away.

"Joie?" He stepped back enough to look at her. "Babe, what's the matter?"

She swallowed hard. He always sensed her moods. Her eyes stung, but she refused to draw attention to her tears by wiping them away. "It—it's awful. They fought."

He reached out, touched her cheek tenderly. "Who fought?"

She told him everything. Recounted how Leigh Ann had arranged for that woman to cover her wedding on her blog, make a show out of everything. She'd resisted, of course. Wouldn't anyone?

Clint remained quiet, simply nodded, urging her on.

"Well, we were in the middle of a heated debate about the whole thing. You know how Leigh Ann can be. And, well—I was having none of it. This is our wedding, not some stinking internet show."

Clint looked confused. "And Karyn and Leigh Ann fought about that?"

"No," she said. "In the heat of our argument, Leigh Ann randomly picked up Karyn's phone when it buzzed alerting there was an incoming text. Karyn had her hands full holding Hudson," she explained.

"That's when everything exploded. Leigh Ann saw a text she wasn't supposed to."

Clint frowned. "What kind of text?"

"A text from Tessa McCreary."

"The realtor?"

Joie nodded. "Yes. We discovered Karyn is selling her house. She plans to move to California, start some kind of restaurant with Zane Keppner's help."

Pain returned to Joie's gut. Sure, she'd lived in Boise for many months, but that was a few hours' drive away. California was like another planet in comparison, no matter how many scheduled flights there were between the two states.

Clint reached for her.

She moved into the circle of his arms, loving the feel of him against her. "Leigh Ann did not react well, to put it lightly. She called Karyn selfish. Karyn surprisingly retaliated, accused Leigh Ann of living out her wedding dreams through me, said she was a vise holding us all in her controlling grip, or some such thing. They were flat-out, cast-iron witches to each other," she whispered against his chest. "They said horrible things."

She wiped her snotty nose against the warm soft cloth of his T-shirt. "I mean, sure—everyone knows Leigh Ann is pushy, and Karyn needs an extra room for all her emotional baggage, but—" She choked up. "I always knew they loved each other."

"They do still love each other," he gently reminded.

Joie shook her head. All her life she'd imagined the love between them all a durable thing, a strong saddle-leather kind of emotion that could handle the wear and tear of any ride, but now she saw how mistaken that perception was. "Yes, but—" Her voice sounded foreign and unsteady. "Something tells me apologies are going to be slow coming—if ever. My sisters may frost over their wounds and move on, but I'm afraid their relationship will forever remain scarred."

16

L eigh Ann snatched the half-used bottle of Clinique foundation from her bathroom cabinet and slammed it into the trash can. She opened a bottle of highlighting serum, sniffed. Even though the container was nearly full, she gave it a hearty toss. Same with some scented antiperspirant and a bottle of cologne that she couldn't recall. She remembered it was a gift but couldn't remember the giver or the occasion.

Systematically, she stripped the tiny shelves of nearly every product, sending them into the trash container with loud bangs. She was ruthless, not taking mercy on even a little box of Q-tips.

The front door slammed. She could hear Mark making his way to the kitchen. Seconds later, his footsteps in the hallway alerted he was heading in her direction.

Satisfied she'd cleared the cabinet of unwanted bottles just taking up space, she picked up the trash can and moved for the door where she nearly collided with her husband.

"Move!" she barked.

Mark held up both hands in surrender. "Hey, what did I do?"

"Nothing. I just need to get this junk out to the street before the garbage collector comes."

Mark ran his hand through his hair, stepped aside. "Okay, sure. But it's really starting to come down out there. In all likelihood, the collectors will be delayed—if they come at all."

This infuriated Leigh Ann even more. She thrust the can into her husband's suited gut. "Well, take this then. Get rid of it."

Confused, Mark gently pulled the trash can from her hands. He set it down. "What's going on?"

"Nothing's going on!" she retorted, then spun and headed for the kitchen.

Mark followed. "Leigh Ann, you need to come clean. Something's up, I can tell."

This time she couldn't keep the tears from forming. Angry tears—hurt tears.

She turned, threw her hands up in the air. "I'm done. Absolutely done!"

Mark was smart enough not to interrupt. He simply nodded, silently urging her on.

"No, I mean it," she said. "I've spent my entire life doing for those two. What do I get in return? They accuse me of being overbearing, of being controlling." She glared at Mark. "Like I said, I'm done."

"Who?"

She shook her head. "What?"

"Who?" he repeated.

Leigh Ann clenched her fists in frustration. "My sisters!"

Mark continued to look confused. He paused as if he wanted to say more but instead held out his arms to her.

The gesture undid her. Her lip quivered. She rapidly blinked her eyes several times to hide her emotion.

"C'mere," he said, inviting her in for a hug. When she didn't immediately move to accept his offer, he reached and pulled her against him, kissed the top of her head. "Look, I don't know what all this is about, but I'm sure it'll all blow over. You three love each other."

"Apparently, not much. Karyn is moving. She didn't deem it important to even tell us before listing her house. It's as if I don't even know her anymore. She took off to California with that Zane guy and returned somebody different." She pulled back, looked at her husband in the face. "Do you think she stopped to think about my feelings? I'm the one who took over her duties at the Sun Valley Lodge so she could even go in the first place. The trip was supposed to be temporary, a chance to get her head together after suffering Grayson dumping her."

"He didn't dump her, Leigh Ann. He left so he could be a full-time father. I'm sure it was very hard for him to make that decision, especially knowing what it would do to Karyn."

"And she isn't stopping to think about what this move will do to us—to Dad and Joie." A fresh set of tears sprouted at the thought of her sister living so far away.

She felt a fluttering of panic. Suddenly, she understood the price of their argument, how everything had fractured—with both Karyn and Joie. For a second, she wished she could take it all back, change the way she'd erupted, the things she'd said in anger. Anything so that she and her sisters were on the same page again.

"Honey, it'll turn out okay. I promise. You'll talk all this through with Karyn and get this misunderstanding resolved. True, you may not change her mind about moving, but if that is how this turns out, you can fly there often."

She blubbered against his shirt. "Why does everyone think the airlines will fix everything?"

"Because it's a viable option. Families who love each other

aren't always able to live near one another. Flying is the next best thing. That, and video conferencing on social media platforms. You'll see—everything will be fine."

He rubbed the tears from her eyes. "How is Joie sitting with all this?"

Leigh Ann audibly groaned. "Joie is mad and refuses to let Croslyn Merritt cover her wedding and feature the ceremony and after-party on Happenings. Brides across America would die for the same opportunity—but no, not Joie. She'd show up to her own wedding in jeans and boots if I let her." She took a deep breath. "That's what started all this in the first place."

The truth crept over Mark's face. He frowned. "Did you ask her before you arranged for all that?"

Leigh Ann's chest tightened. Of course, she hadn't asked. She shouldn't have to. What harm could it possibly be for the wedding to be featured in such an honorable manner in one of the most lauded forums online?

"You didn't," he guessed, without needing her to respond. "Look, I can maybe understand—"

"Oh, don't you start too," she told him, feeling attacked again. "You know I only have both of my sisters' best interests in mind when I make any decisions that affect them. I've done that since they were both tiny."

Her ragged heart skipped a beat. A sudden tide of memories flooded her mind. Fleeting images, remembered moments.

Joie, her long brown hair tangled and dripping wet, her knees drawn up to her chest, her fingers plowing through the dirt out behind the barn, looking for hidden treasures—laughing, always laughing. Karyn lying belly-down on her bed with her nose in a book. Eyes red with emotion from some story and a pile of used tissues wadded next to her.

She and Mark stared long and hard at each other. Deep inside, she wanted to admit she'd screwed up. Yet a small voice in the back of her mind whispered that it was she who had been terribly wronged. She had nothing to apologize for.

She believed that with every ounce of her being. Even so, a tiny sob rose in her throat.

She'd never felt so alone.

17

"Well, hey—I'm sure looking forward to seeing you, bro." Clint leaned against the counter in Joie's dad's kitchen. "We'll see you in the morning."

He hung up his phone with a wide smile on his face, then grabbed a can of Dr Pepper off the counter and joined Joie and her dad at the nearby dining table. "That was Mike. His flight gets in tomorrow."

"How long since you've seen your brother?" Joie asked as she lifted Hudson, who had just finished his bottle, to her shoulder and began patting his back. Her baby was the perfect diet plan, helping her drop a few pounds before the big day. Seemed he was always hungry when she sat down to eat.

Clint looked toward the ceiling, mentally calculating the time span. "Gosh, over a year." He slid into a chair next to Joie. "Anyway, I'm really excited to see him."

Joie's dad scooped a bite of pancake dripping in syrup onto his fork. "Older or younger?"

"Younger by two years." Clint picked up his fork. "It was just the two of us, and we were pretty tight growing up. Always found a way to have fun." He cut into a link sausage, held the bite in midair. "Once, we went camping over at Caddo Lake, not far from the Louisiana border. We pitched our tent in a special spot we'd found underneath a canopy of cypress draped with Spanish moss with big plans to fish for some trophy large-mouth bass at daybreak."

He laughed. "Unfortunately, we ran into some unexpected visitors."

Joie's eyes grew wide. "Oh, no. I don't want to hear any snake stories."

Clint dropped his fork to his plate and wiped at the corners of his mouth with his napkin. "No snakes. Wild boar."

Her dad leaned forward in his chair. "I've heard the state of Texas allows you to hunt those feral pigs without a license, no limits on the kill."

Clint nodded. "Yeah, without some sort of check, the population would take over, and wild pigs are very destructive—and they are mean as spit." He chuckled. "You don't want to find yourself face-to-face with a seven-hundred-pound hog without a gun in your hand."

He grabbed his coffee mug, took a quick sip before continuing. "But, that's exactly what happened that night. I had to take a leak and stepped away from camp, soon learning I wasn't alone."

Joie's eyebrows lifted. "What did you do?"

"I tried standing very still. Didn't matter—that hog's eyes reflected the campfire and slowly started moving for me. I knew any minute the blasted thing would charge. No doubt, I was had. That is, until Mike dropped the pig with one shot. He likes to remind me often how he saved my life that night. Tells me I owe him—and he makes me pay up every time we see each other. He just reminded me on the phone of the debt and suggested I pay for all his drinks while he's here." Clint shoved the bite of link sausage into his mouth and chewed, still smiling. "I never took a leak in the woods again without taking my gun with me."

"That's a great story," her dad said. "And I love that you and your brother are so close. That's the way it is with my girls, right Joie?"

An uncomfortable silence filled the room. Joie and Clint glanced at each another.

Her dad laid down his fork. "Okay, what's up?"

Guilt flooded as Joie took a deep breath, released it, and looked at her father. "We—uh, we ran into a little trouble with the wedding."

Her dad's eyebrows furrowed. "Trouble?"

She looked to Clint for support. He nodded for her to go on. She looked across the table to her dad. "Well, what happened is this. Leigh Ann pimped my wedding out on some women's blog."

"Blog?"

"That's a kind of online magazine—on the internet," she explained.

Her dad drew his own deep breath. "Oh, I see."

"Without clearing it with us first," she rushed to add, nervously patting her baby's back a little faster. "And when I threw a fit, it turned into a confrontation of sorts."

"Okay," her dad said. "You guys often rub each other wrong. You'll fix it."

She tried to look calm and composed, but inside her gut was roiling. "That's not all."

Concern crossed her father's face. "Oh?"

"Yeah, well—that's really the minor issue. In the middle of our heated conversation, Leigh Ann picked up Karyn's phone and saw a text from her realtor."

Her father nodded. "Oh," he said. "She hadn't had the chance to tell you yet."

Joie stopped patting Hudson's back. "You knew?"

Her dad nodded. "We'd had several conversations about it. I was the one who counseled she wait to tell you girls until after the wedding. I can see I was wrong to give that advice."

"Leigh Ann blew up. Maybe because she was already mad at me for telling her she couldn't make my wedding into a circus. I mean, she really let Karyn have it. Karyn uncharacteristically defended herself. I was a bit proud of her, frankly. But they both said horrid things to one another." She swallowed to keep tears from forming. "It's bad, Dad. And it's only two days until the wedding." She looked at her father, helplessly. "I don't know what to do."

Her dad looked at Clint, then back at her. "Well, I suspected Leigh Ann would have a hard time with Karyn's decision, but that's no call for ugliness with one another."

She got scared then, seeing the look of concern on her father's face. "I'm not sure this is going to just blow over, Dad. And certainly not before the wedding."

Joie felt herself tensing when he didn't say anything for several seconds. It was clear he was thinking.

Finally, he looked directly at her, cleared his throat. "Relationships—especially the important ones—aren't easy to maintain. Often because the relationship is comprised of broken people. The best thing you girls can do is to extend a measure of grace to one another—and forgive." He paused. "I'll be asking the good Lord to soften all your hearts."

18

A small crowd gathered tightly around a television monitor mounted on the wall inside Bistro on Fourth. Nash Billingsley joined them, wiping his hands on a towel. His faithful dog, Chelsea, was at his feet, tail wagging.

"What's all this?" he said.

"Shhh," Lucy tucked a pencil in her blonde hair and wiped the last crumbs off a red checker-clothed table nearby. "We're trying to hear the weather report."

"A potentially historic storm with predicted driving blizzard conditions and thundersnow it's expected in the Wood River Valley. The unexpected storm threatens residents and vacationers in the Sun Valley area over the next couple of days. Snowfall rates are predicted to be in excess of three inches per hour, with accumulation of more than two and a half feet, and will bring strong wind gusts in excess of fifty miles per hour." The reporter's face took on a serious look. *"Prepare now for this severe winter storm."*

Before anyone could react, the front door flew open and in swept Trudy Dilworth, waving her arms. "Have you heard? Have you heard?"

Lucy flipped the wet cloth onto her shoulder and pulled the pen from her hair. "The weather? Sounds like a real stinker of a storm."

Miss Trudy parked her fists on her ample hips. "No, not the storm. Have you heard what happened between the Abbott girls? They had a big fight. The kind of fight that could threaten the wedding." She shook her head, made a *tsking* sound. "I've been looking forward to this celebration ever since that trial." She clasped her pudgy fingers in an almost prayer-like pose. "Everything about Clint professing his abiding love for Joie up on that witness stand, then proposing to her—" She fluttered her eyelashes. "It was all so romantic. I just couldn't wait to see them pledge themselves to each other at their wonderful wedding—and now this!" she cried. "I heard the wedding has been called off!"

"The wedding is called off?" Dee Dee Hamilton moved from the crowd and walked over to Miss Trudy. "I'm doing all the flowers. Surely, I would have heard something from Leigh Ann."

Elda Vaughn set her blue mug on the counter, looking like she was going to cry. "I bought a new dress for the occasion. Where did you hear this?"

Miss Trudy shook her head. "From an excellent source. Margaret Manley, who is best friends with Paula Martin, the gift store manager at the lodge—well, she overheard her talking with her son, who is a box boy at Atkinson's Market. He heard Mark talking with Leigh Ann on the phone about everything."

The group sadly nodded. "That's too bad," one of them said.

Nash flipped the towel onto his shoulder. "I'm not sure that means the wedding is called off."

Elda looked hopeful. "That's right."

Miss Trudy leaned forward. "Well, that's not the worst of it. It has something to do with Karyn moving. I heard Leigh Ann didn't take the news well and blew up. Karyn changed her mind about staying with Leigh Ann. Instead, she packed up and moved back to her own house. I drove by her place this morning, hoping to catch her home. Tess McCreary's realtor sign was in the front yard—with a sold banner pasted across it."

There was a collective intake of air followed by a groan.

Dee Dee's hand went to her chest. "Karyn's moving?"

The news seemed to take everyone by surprise, especially Nash. "Man, I'm sorry to hear that. I always liked that girl. She'll be missed around here."

Lucy adjusted the waistline of her too-tight jeans. "As juicy as all this gossip is, and y'all know I love gossip, none of this speculation matters. Fight, or no fight. Ain't no wedding going to take place with that storm on top of us."

JOIE STOOD in front of Leigh Ann's door. Every passing minute tightened something in her until she began to think that she might break apart. There was a lot riding on this visit.

She lifted her hand to ring the doorbell. The door swung open.

Leigh Ann looked her over. "What are you doing just standing out there like that?"

"Don't get snitty. I came to fix things."

Leigh Ann tentatively stepped back. "Oh, and how do you propose that happens?"

Joie pushed past her. "Give it a rest, Leigh Ann. You should be the one coming to me, but I'm here. That counts for something."

Leigh Ann didn't look so sure. "Did you hear about the big storm on its way?" she said, safely avoiding a direct response.

"We have to fix this." Joie gave her a look that said she wasn't here to play games.

Leigh Ann stood with her arms folded. Finally, she softened. "Yes," she conceded. "We do."

Joie thought about what her dad had said. That, coupled with Clint's urging, and she was here. Might as well jump off the cliff, so to speak. "Look, you can let that lady do a write-up. A small one," she clarified. "And no pictures of us. Just the venue."

Leigh Ann opened her mouth to argue. "But—"

"But nothing. Take it—or leave it." Joie drilled her with a look. "That's as far as I'm going to budge."

Her sister stubbornly frowned. "Fine."

"And you have to go say you're sorry to Karyn," Joie quickly added. "Take back the mean things you said."

"Oh no!" Leigh Ann waved her off. "She's the one who—"

"Or Clint and I will take Dad and Hudson and go elope."

Leigh Ann looked skeptical. "In this weather?"

"There's no magic to getting married day after tomorrow. We can wait it out, you know." She hoped her threat didn't sound hollow and unconvincing.

Leigh Ann's expression announced she clearly felt hemmed in, trapped. "Only if Karyn will mutually apologize, and drop this silly motion of moving."

Joie couldn't believe her sister was being so stubborn, so ridiculously unreasonable. This was a new one level of control, even for Leigh Ann. She was disappointed with Karyn's decision as well, but she had every right to live somewhere else if she so chose.

"Listen to me, Leigh Ann. I know it's going to be hard for us to adjust to Karyn not living here. I'm as saddened by the news as you are. Believe me. But we don't have the right to dictate where she calls home."

"Sun Valley will always be her home," Leigh Ann argued.

"Yes, and she'd be back here often. You know that. But what good does it do to try and make her feel bad for trying to change her life a little? We both know how hard it's been for her since Dean's death. She had little reserve to accommodate the betrayal she felt when Grayson moved back to Alaska and that relationship ended. We need to cut her some slack, you know?"

Leigh Ann could be a tough nut to crack. Given any other circumstance, she would never have made the effort to come over here and mend things. She'd even folded and let Leigh Ann have her own way, for goodness sakes. The least her sister could do was extend the same to Karyn.

"So, c'mon—it's my wedding in two days. You have to get past this with Karyn."

For a moment, Joie believed she was getting through to her sister. Yet, clearly, Leigh Ann was struggling.

"I'll—well, I'll think about it. That's all I can promise right now," she said, trying to smile.

But it was false, that smile. Her eyes said something else entirely.

19

L eigh Ann felt her recurring headache coming on as she pulled on her snow boots. Vowing to take two aspirin as soon as she was in the car, she waved goodbye to the girls at the spa and made her way outside and trudged through freshly fallen snow to her car. Clearly, the massage had failed to loosen her tight neck muscles.

She was surprised to see how much snow had accumulated. Retailers were having a difficult time keeping the sidewalks clear. Snowplows were making more frequent passes on the main roadways but could barely keep up. If she was going to stop by Karyn's on her way home, she'd better make it quick.

Leigh Ann unlocked her car door and slipped inside, turned on the heater to let it run while she scraped off the snow from her windshield. While she loved living in a ski resort town, she couldn't help but miss summer right now.

When she'd finished, she returned to her car, pulled off her gloves, and turned on the radio before pulling out onto the roadway.

"A blizzard event is expected in the next twelve to thirty-six hours. Sustained wind or frequent gusts will limit air travel and

blowing snow is predicted to reduce visibility to less than a quarter mile and will accompany accumulating falling snow of close to three feet."

She sighed and turned down the volume. These out-of-town forecasters made a living reporting weather drama. How often had they made it sound like Armageddon was on its way, only to wake to a fresh foot of snow that gave the ski hills their glorious reputation for powder? Still, she knew Clint's brother was flying in and hoped his flight would not be delayed, or worse, canceled. Flying into Friedman could be tricky anyway, but low visibility always played havoc.

No weather event would dare interfere with this wedding! She'd spent entirely too many hours planning and working to make everything perfect. Besides, the real storm she had to worry about was just ahead.

Feeling a twinge of nervousness, Leigh Ann gripped the steering wheel a little tighter.

Leigh Ann could drive the route to Karyn's house with her eyes closed, but today she chose a different, longer route. Possibly to add time to gather her thoughts.

She couldn't remember a time when she and Karyn had fought. As kids, they'd gotten on each other's nerves over the typical things—lids left off the toothpaste, borrowing favorite sweaters without asking, and such. But, never had they been this angry with each other.

Leigh Ann felt a recurring stab of resentment.

How could Karyn not see how hurtful her decision was? Especially given she'd failed to even consult with her, or anyone in the family, before making such a life change. They'd always been so close. Such disregard for her feelings really hurt. They'd talked daily on the phone for years, up until Karyn took her motorcycle trip—and even then, they visited frequently. In light of that, she couldn't mention any of this?

The thought of not only her sister, but her best friend,

moving that far away left her feeling small and dry. Who would she shop with? Who would drop by and have coffee? Sure, she had friends like Dee Dee, but she had to get dressed before they came over. Karyn was different. They were sisters.

And that was the crux of the matter, right there.

Leigh Ann was heartbroken by Karyn's decision to move away. She'd miss her sister terribly. For the life of her, she couldn't understand why Karyn didn't feel the same.

Then there were those horrible things her sister had said. Karyn had suggested she lived such a pitiful a life that she had to create happiness by forcing herself into her the lives of those she loved. How dare she claim that all she did for her family was motivated by nothing but self-interest!

Feeling defensive, Leigh Ann lifted her chin. She'd had every right to set her straight.

Suddenly, the rear end of her car swerved. She tapped the brakes carefully, and slowed to a crawl. The slick roads were definitely becoming an issue. She made a mental note to have Mark put on the tire chains if things got worse.

Oh! And she'd have to make sure to double the runs the Zamboni would make at the ice skating rink. She wanted everything perfect for Joie's wedding. And that was *not* because she was a bored housewife. All this effort was to create a night both Clint and Joie would remember forever.

Minutes later, filled with resolve, she pulled up to Karyn's house. She'd fall on her sword and try to make peace, but she was like a dog with a bone and the truth was she wasn't done chewing on her effort to change Karyn's mind. Surely there was something she could say to keep her sister from messing up both their lives.

If Karyn went through with her plan to move to California, it would be like shoving their close relationship down Baldy Mountain on skis without any poles. Most certainly, they would both tumble and crash.

Some would claim she was being over-dramatic. She made a sound—a kind of snort. Perhaps they'd be right, but that was not what really mattered.

She worked up a smile. Those people didn't know how close she and Karyn really were—how sure she was that, in the end, she could make Karyn see things differently. She could simply change her mind and cancel the listing. If she wanted to start a restaurant, Mark would help her—here.

She negotiated a sharp turn and eased the car up into Karyn's driveway. There it was again, that nervousness.

She turned off the key and got out of the car, tightened her scarf around her neck to keep the cold air from climbing down her back. That's when she spotted it. A sign posted in Karyn's snowy front yard.

SOLD.

Without a word, she turned and got back in her car—drove away.

20

I t was no secret to Joie or anyone else, that more snow had fallen in Sun Valley in the past week than in the entire preceding winter season. Storms had lined up and taken aim at the tiny Idaho town, one after the other, leaving everyone, including Joie, shaking their heads wondering when the snowfall would stop.

Even the most seasoned weathercasters hesitated to predict when the snowfall would subside. While residents of Sun Valley were used to storms, actually applauded snowfall—inches translated to money in this town—this storm was far outside the norm. All of Leigh Ann's carefully detailed wedding plans wouldn't matter. Regardless of what the celebration, it was entirely possible no one would risk driving, given the horrible conditions that were developing outside.

Outside the barn window, snow blew in a horizontal blur. "Boy, it doesn't look good out there." She pulled little Hudson closer, tucked the blanket around his tiny body.

Her dad gave her an encouraging look. "I know you're concerned about all the wedding plans, but worrying won't change a thing."

Joie would love to rein in her thoughts, but self-control had never been her strong suit. She held up her phone. "Leigh Ann won't pick up. Bet she's having a fit right about now."

"Cell service tends to be a bit spotty when these storms hit," her dad reminded. "All of us have to believe everything will turn out the way the good Lord intends, including your sister. And I'm not just talking about wedding plans."

Clint snapped a lead rope onto the nylon halter and led her dad's mare into a stall lined with fresh straw. He unhooked the rope, patted the horse's hind quarter. "There you go, girl." He closed the stall door and joined them at the front of the barn. "Well, that should do it."

Her dad's weathered hands slid the heavy interior barn door shut. "Thanks for your help, Clint."

"No problem. Do you think we should place a couple more heat lamps? I have plenty in at the stables in town and can spare some if you need."

Edwin moved to the pot-bellied stove located by the entrance. He rubbed his hands in front of the wood stove, warming his deeply calloused palms. "I think we're good to go. You guys were a big help."

"Does Sebastian need help with the feeding tonight?" Clint asked while pulling on his gloves.

"Shouldn't. When storm predictions started rolling in, we stacked extra bales outside all the barns and tarped them. We also have hay piled up in all the lambing sheds. If we run out, we've always got the sleigh to transport more." Her dad slipped his gloves back on. "What's the situation with your brother?"

"Looks like all incoming planes have been grounded, at least for the time being." Clint took Hudson from Joie's arms. "It's not likely he's going to make it here in time."

Edwin patted his shoulder. "We'll keep that situation in our prayers as well."

Joie felt her heart tug. She knew Clint was terribly disappointed. She also knew he always looked at the bright side of things. She loved that about him.

She joined them at the stove, basked in the heat that emanated from the embers burning inside.

She wished she could be as upbeat as her husband-to-be. Unfortunately, there was little to be happy about when there loomed a very real possibility her wedding would be snowed out. While she'd resisted all the hoopla initially, now that the big day was nearly here, she had to admit how much she looked forward to pledging her life to Clint. Right after their vows, he would adopt little Hudson. She also had to admit she looked forward to seeing Clint's face when he spotted her in that gown.

Now, everything she was anticipating was threatened by this interminable storm.

At least that blogger lady's camera team would also not be able to fly in for the ceremony, she told herself in consolation.

Her dad bent to move a sack of pellets out of the way. "Why don't you two head for the house. I'm going to throw some more wood in the stove, then I'll be right behind you."

Joie nodded reluctantly. "Okay, but don't be long."

Together, she and Clint exited the barn through a side door leading to the main house. Even in the driving snow, the landscape was a fairy-tale world, child-like and funny. Boughs of trees adorned with thick pillows of snow, the ground a series of humps and mounds, beneath which underbrush or outcrops of rock lay hidden; a mural of white.

The landscape seemed foreign, even a bit disorienting. Snow drifts had blown up on the front porch. Even the rocking chairs were mounded with snow. With his boot, Clint worked to clear the drifts out of the way so the front door could be opened.

Joie held little Hudson close. She bit her lip, knowing her dad was right. There was no sense pining for what she couldn't change. If necessary, they'd simply reschedule the wedding to the following weekend.

It had only been a little over a day and she already missed the constant telephone calls with her sisters, their chats about all the small things—the speeding ticket she got last week, what color Leigh Ann wanted to paint her bathroom walls, whether the novel Karyn had read deserved to be on the *New York Times* bestseller list.

She longed for the memories of last summer, when she and her sisters sat in those empty rocking chairs—and everything was right with the world. No one was mad. Well, Leigh Ann was on her case, but that was normal.

Inside, she handed little Hudson off into Clint's arms. "You okay?" he asked.

Joie watched Clint place her son on the sofa. He unwrapped the blanket and went to work extricating him from his thick coat and his furry little hat.

"I need to talk to you," she told him, remembering the prenup. They might not get another few minutes alone before tomorrow night.

"I'm listening." He handed Hudson back to her, then took off his own jacket and hung it on the coat tree next to the door.

"I've got something I need you to sign—a prenuptial agreement of sorts."

Clint raised his eyebrows. "Of sorts?"

Joie rushed to explain. "Yes. It outlines what happens to my portion of the law firm if anything should happen—I mean, just in case. That's all. I don't have much else really."

Clint moved to her, turned her to face him. He tucked a strand of hair behind her ear, looked earnestly into her eyes. "Don't marry me unless this is a forever thing."

"Oh, it is—I mean, I'll never do anything to end my marriage—but Maddy suggested we cover all the bases."

Clint drilled her with a puzzled look. "This is no baseball

game, Joie. There's no need to cover any bases." There was a slight shift in the air.

An uneasiness prickled Joie's skin. She'd failed to explain adequately, had offended him. "Clint, listen—this is forever for me too. But there are all kinds of business reasons for partners to have these kinds of documents in place. Maddy needs protection. The document not only covers what happens in the event of marriage dissolution, but what happens if I die and my estate suddenly owns half of her business." She watched his face closely to see if her words had any impact.

A half-moon smile slowly appeared on his handsome face. "Okay. Makes sense. I'll sign your prenup—provided you sign something I need."

A slow breath leaked from between Joie's lips. She didn't know what she had been expecting, but not that. "You need something signed?"

"Wait here." Clint swept past her, headed back to the coat tree. He dug in the pocket of his coat and retrieved a badly wrinkled envelope. He lifted the unglued flap and pulled out a single page document, walked it over and handed it to her. "I need you to sign this."

Joie gave him a puzzled look, but his head was down. He wouldn't look at her.

Stunned into silence, she lifted the document and carefully read it.

Tears sprouted. "Clint? This is a trust agreement."

"Yes," he confirmed, still not looking at her.

"You—I mean, why didn't you tell me?" Her mouth went dry. She could barely breathe. "You have assets? I mean, a lot of assets?"

He finally looked at her. "Yes. My grandfather was William Buckley Ladner, a name that's pretty well known in Texas. Grandpa was a college dropout who once had a job fixing broken televisions. He built wealth by picking up distressed assets such as bonds backed by airplanes after 9/11, then cashing out at a profit."

Joie swallowed. "Two point four billion in profit?"

Clint looked embarrassed. "Yeah. He did pretty well."

Joie lifted the document into the air. "But why didn't you tell me? I mean, why are you managing a stable in Sun Valley if you have all this money?"

"It's all in that trust." He pointed to the document. "Besides, no one can serve two masters. The way I see it, it's far too easy to fall in love with wealth and lose yourself in the process. I'm not defined by how much money I have in the bank, like most people would consider."

She didn't know what to say to that. True, had she known, she would have thought of him differently. Likely, she would never have invited any sort of relationship with a man that wealthy. "Well, this news is a little overwhelming, I have to admit."

That made him smile. "Yeah, but it doesn't have to be a big deal. Like I said, the money is in a trust. This document makes you equal trustee with the entire amount passing to Hudson and our future kiddos."

"What about your brother?"

"Mike owns a duplicate trust in his own name," he explained. "Although my investments have done a little better." His face broke into a slight grin. "Anyway, it's all yours—ours, whatever."

His words smacked her with the force of a two-by-four, stealing her breath. Humiliation filled her.

How could he possibly love her like that? She had a habit of withholding. He gave her everything he had, in more ways than one.

Her independent streak had rebelled against ever wanting to be rescued from her propensity to run smack dab into trouble. After her relationship fiasco with a married man, she'd never wanted to need Clint or any man.

She shook her head, unable to believe how he'd been by her side the entire time, offering encouragement and consolation.

And now this.

Tears formed as she reached for his hand. "How do you do it?" she asked. "How do you love me when I'm unlovable? How do you stand by my side when I don't deserve it? How can you possibly offer me all you have, when I—"

His hand went to her chin, and he gently lifted her face. "True love isn't earned, Joie. It's a gift."

Joie touched the crest of his cheek, then traced the edges of his jawline to the cleft in his chin. His skin was warm and rough against her fingers. She felt a stirring inside.

She didn't deserve his love, but she'd gladly accept it.

Wedding, or none—she didn't need a ceremony, because at that moment, she gave him her whole heart, forever.

21

K aryn opened the kitchen drawer and scooped the contents, among them a whisk, a vegetable peeler, a garlic press, and an ice cream scoop, all into a waiting box. She closed the packed cardboard container with strapping tape, then lugged the heavy box over to the window and stacked it on top of the others.

The news her house had sold so quickly had taken her by surprise. Even more, that the buyers, a couple from New Jersey, wanted to close in ten days.

It seemed like only yesterday that she and Dean had signed the papers to buy this house. She'd worried they couldn't afford a place overlooking the golf course, especially in the heart of Sun Valley.

Dean had assured her he had everything taken care of. Soon, she learned his parents had provided a substantial down payment as a wedding gift.

Her former in-laws had taken the news about her move much better than expected. Of course, Bert and Aggie lived in California much of the year. As Aggie pointed out, they'd still see each other frequently. Still, they'd urged her to keep her house in Sun Valley. "You have so many memories there," Aggie reminded. "You may be sorry you closed the door on that part of your life."

Karyn gently explained that, while those memories would always remain dear to her heart, the day-to-day reminders of everything she'd lost had grown too much to bear. Her life had become a quagmire of broken dreams. She was ready to be free.

Her friend, Zane Keppner, helped her discover a neoteric truth.

"Everyone is broken," he'd told her. "At some time or another, you will experience a hit in life that tears you wide open. An event that will change you completely."

It was true. Life after felt more fragile, far more vulnerable. She was now aware of dangers in life, yet also of the beauty in it.

Zane helped her to understand that being broken was a given. But what she did after the break was totally up to her.

"Many will stay shattered," he explained. "They'll let their battered and bruised heart and mind lie there bleeding on the floor. They'll become jaded and bitter and angry that they'd been broken in the first place."

There was a trace of a smile on his face as he took her hand. "They refuse to see that we're all that way—that the game of life often deals a difficult hand." He paused. "Others though— others will make something of their broken selves. They'll find strength in the fractures. They'll get up off the floor and allow the world to see their changed, broken, vulnerable selves."

He squeezed her hand. "And it's magical. You know why?"

Zane shared a look that spoke volumes.

"Because people everywhere are hungry to be shown how to get up and find that kind of strength. They're literally dying to learn how to rise up. Granted, the floor is comfortable. Anger and bitterness are seductive, and folks are convincing when it comes to using brokenness as an excuse to quit in life."

There had been an awkward pause. Zane, never one to back away from a difficult conversation, looked her directly in the eyes. "Karyn, you need to show people what you're made of. Get your butt off the floor, wipe your wounds, and raise your voice. Tell us who you are and what you will become from your brokenness." Another brief pause, and then, "Do this, so you can lead the way and show others how to pick themselves up and live. Then, my friend, your days will have meaning again. Take your life back—make it matter."

Karyn absorbed every word and had taken his message to heart. She had a way to transform her life and give it new purpose.

She would be brave.

After much consideration, she'd decided to follow a quiet dream she'd put on the shelf years ago. With Zane's help, she would open an eatery in the tiny Northern California town of St. Helena, using rented space from Zane's good friend, Ann Riggin.

No longer would she sit in her house and pine the hours away reminiscing about life with Dean, and Grayson. She would cease living in the past and would embrace a new adventure. The prospect so excited her she could barely sleep at night.

Something deep inside told her this would make Dean proud.

The sound of a car door slamming outside interrupted her reverie. Startled, she glanced at the kitchen clock. It was a little after ten. The only person she knew who would stop by at this hour without calling first was Leigh Ann, and it was highly unlikely her angry sister would be dropping in for a friendly visit.

Before Karyn moved for the door, she paused at the window and peered out into the darkness. The person standing in the porchlight was indeed her older sister.

Although it was hard to tell with her wearing a thick parka and fur-lined hood.

"Leigh Ann?" she said, swinging the door open before her sister could ring the doorbell. "What are you doing here? Do you know what time it is?"

Her sister pulled the hood from her head, sending snow fluttering to the floor. "Of course, I know what time it is." From her tone, she was clearly not over her pout.

Admittedly, neither was she.

"Why are you here?" Karyn asked as she slid the door closed behind her sister.

Ignoring the question, Leigh Ann strode into the entry foyer, removed her coat, and hung it in the coat closet. "While I'd much rather be on a flight to Fiji with Mark, my suitcase packed with swimsuits and sandals, I have a wedding to put on. Despite my personal feelings, I follow through on my commitments. Family comes first."

The sharp edge in her sister's voice made Karyn wince. "That's what they say," she said, annoyed at the defensiveness she heard in her own voice.

When would she stop giving other people power over her emotions?

Leigh Ann moved on into the house, taking in the living room as though she were seeing it for the first time. "I see you've already started packing."

Karyn nodded. "Yes, we close in less than ten days."

The news was clearly distressing. "Oh?" The forced smile Leigh Ann gave her was almost that of a stranger's—not the one she loved, that crinkled up her eyes and made her smile back.

Despite her conviction to divorce herself from the drama her sister had created, Karyn's insides wavered. Some roads led to bad places and a small voice told her she might want to turn around before everything went off a cliff.

"Have you eaten? Dinner, I mean?"

"Of course, I have. It's ten o'clock at night." Leigh Ann marched into the kitchen, placed her hands on her hips. She looked around at the boxes.

Without another word, she grabbed one and headed for a cupboard, opened the door. "Don't just stand there," she said, taking a stack of plates from the shelf. "We've got a lot to do. We have to get you packed, and then we have a wedding to put on."

22

Nearly three and a half feet of snow had dropped overnight, leaving Sun Valley residents waking to closed roadways and partial power outages. Shelves at Atkinson's Market were nearly bare, and a person would be hard-pressed to find a case of bottled water to purchase. With more storms predicted over the next hours, everyone was warned to remain inside.

This was not the news Joie had wanted to learn on the morning of her wedding. Leigh Ann was not happy about the situation either. She called even before a hint of dawn broke over the mountains.

"Are you listening to the weather reports?" Leigh Ann's voice was shrill, the level of high-pitched, thin sound that signaled her sister was about to go over the edge. "I don't know what we're going to do. Power is out at the lodge, and last-minute deliveries are an absolute no-go! This is a crisis, Joie. How are we going to pull off a wedding when snow drifts nearly seven-feet high have to be shoveled from the front of the church for guests to even get inside the front door?"

"Calm down," Joie told her. "We can't control any of this. We'll just have to reschedule."

"Do you have any idea—I mean, *any* idea—what kind of planning goes into an event like this? Flowers don't just show up; they have to be ordered weeks in advance. Venue dates have to be cleared. There isn't another date available at the lodge for weeks, perhaps more than a month. How do you even notify the guests? Email, I suppose. But what about flights? And the cake? What are we going to do with all that cake?" She groaned under the weight of all the implications. "You can't just blink your eyes and make everything come together without nearly starting the process entirely over."

A dull ache formed in Joie's stomach. Sure, she wasn't initially thrilled with everything Leigh Ann had planned, but she'd gotten onboard—eventually beginning to look forward to the big day. She was anxious to become Mrs. Clint Ladner and to have Hudson's adoption secured.

"I'm not happy about any of this either, Leigh Ann." She rubbed her forehead. "Look, let me at least get a cup of coffee down me before I have to decide what course to take. It's evident the wedding plans are off. Let's at least start there."

She could hear voices in the kitchen. Her dad was already up.

"Look, I'll call you in an hour or so. We'll figure something out then." Joie clicked off her phone. She slipped from the bed, pulled her robe on, and headed for the kitchen where she found her dad talking with Clint. He held Hudson in his arms.

"Goodness, I didn't even hear him wake up," she said, reaching for her little son.

"No worries. I heard him when I came over to talk to your dad. Took a while to traverse that deep snow. We really got dumped on last night."

Her dad placed his coffee mug on the counter. "We sure did, and the radio is reporting the storm created a lot of havoc. The power is off in much of the valley. It's going to be hours before the snow plows can clear the roadways."

Her father's cell phone rang. He picked up, brought it to his ear as he went to fill his coffee mug back up. At that moment, the lights flickered. Then it went dark.

"Hold on, I'll get candles." She pushed little Hudson back into Clint's arms and moved for the kitchen cupboard where the candles were stored. The light emanating from the fireplace provided barely enough light to see as her hands rummaged the shelves. "Here they are," she announced, pulling down the plastic container. She opened the lid and pulled out several candles, then struck a match, lit each one and carefully placed them on the counter and in the living room.

Her dad stood by the sink, still talking into his phone. She could see a look of concern on his face.

"Dad, what is it?"

He motioned for her to wait by lifting an open palm. "Okay, sure. Sebastian and I will bring the sleigh and horses in. I have a bunch of tarps and some sheets of plywood."

He ended the call with a solemn look. "There's been a partial roof collapse at the church."

Joie's hand went to her chest. "Oh no! How bad?"

"The chapel is fine but the offices are ruined. We need to get in there and help get some protection up until repairs can be made." He looked to Clint. "On second thought, I think I'd best leave Sebastian here to look after the livestock. Would you be able to help out?"

Clint assured him he would. "I think Joie and the baby should go in with us. We don't know how long this storm is going to last and I don't want us separated." He looked to her. "We'll stay with one of your sisters."

Her dad nodded. You can ride on the sleigh with me. I'll have Clint follow us with one of the snowmobiles." He stirred some sugar into his coffee. "We should have replaced the roof on the church years ago, but the congregation elected to use the extra funds for a mission trip to Peru, hoping the roof would last a few more seasons. We all thought the decision was the right one at the time, but we're paying the price now. Of course, none of us expected a snowfall like this."

Joie turned for the hallway. "I'll go pack us a bag."

It wasn't until she'd pulled the small suitcase down from the top shelf of the closet in her old room that she realized no one had even mentioned the wedding.

23

Karyn woke to a frantic call from Melissa Jacquard, the desk clerk at the Sun Valley Lodge. "Karyn, I need help here."

Karyn rubbed her eyes and glanced out the darkness outside her window. "What time is it?"

"It's early, but I can't reach Jon or Leigh Ann. There's no electricity. The generator is failing to come on. It's getting cold in here and people are calling the desk complaining."

"Okay, calm down." She slipped the covers back and brought her feet to the floor, slipped them into her slippers, and grabbed her robe off the bottom of the bed to ward off the chill that brushed her bare shoulders. "I just woke up. Let me get my bearings."

"Then you haven't heard?"

Karyn frowned as she turned on the lamp. Nothing. "Heard what?" She clicked the lamp again. Still nothing.

Melissa was nearly breathless as she explained. "The weather dumped over three feet of snow overnight."

"What?" Karyn knew it was blizzarding when she finally crawled into bed last night, but this was not expected. Even the direst predictions had not warned about this amount of snow-fall. "Are you kidding?"

"No. Roads are all closed. Electricity is out. We have snow-drifts against the front doors that reach halfway up the glass. We can't even get the doors open."

Melissa had her attention now. She climbed from bed and felt her way to the bureau, counted three drawers down in the dark, and pulled a pair of jeans from inside. "I'm on my way," she told her, despite the fact she didn't know how she was going to get there exactly with the roads closed.

"That's not even the worst. One of the kitchen staff told me the roof on the church partially collapsed.

"I'll call Dad. He can bring the snowmobiles in town so we can get around. Look, I'll be there when I can. Until then, gather any staff and build fires in all the fireplaces. Unfortu-nately, only the suites have fireplaces, but any guests that can't keep warm in their rooms can gather in the lobby. Call Amelio. He lives in the condos off Dollar Road, not far. Ask him to get there as soon as possible. We'll have to feed everyone. And Melissa?"

"Yes?"

"Keep me posted."

Karyn scrambled to get dressed. Using the flashlight feature on her phone, she hurried to the kitchen and pulled out candles. Her packing would have to wait. It was going to be a long day.

She quickly jumped in the chilly shower and got dressed, tied her wet hair back in a ponytail. She grabbed her phone and called Leigh Ann.

"I guess you've heard. We have trouble at the lodge."

"Yes, Melissa called right after she talked to you. Appar-ently, she'd been trying to reach me, but I was on the phone with Joie. She thinks the wedding needs to be postponed, but she has no idea—"

"Leigh Ann—"

"No one seems to understand the effort it takes to put on an event like this. We can't simply reschedule. I mean—"

"Leigh Ann!" Karyn shouted.

"You don't have to shout. I heard you," Leigh Ann told her, clearly smarting. "I just—"

Karyn groaned inside. "Leigh Ann, given the circumstances, the wedding will have to be rescheduled. We must focus on the matters at hand. Serious issues must be addressed at the lodge. The church roof has caved and Dad and some men are heading there to take whatever remedial action they can to salvage what remains. Unfortunately, the roadways are impassable. Dad and Clint are on their way. Dad is bringing the sleigh and team of horses, and Clint is driving the snowmobile. It'll be our only transportation." She paused, hoping what she was telling her sister was sinking in. "Leigh Ann, I'm sorry. Both the church and the lodge are now unavailable. The wedding is off. At least for tonight."

There was a heavy pause on the other end of the phone. "Off?"

"Yes. No wedding." Karyn shook her head. You would think Leigh Ann was the one who was supposed to say her nuptials tonight.

"Does Joie know?"

"I'll call her as soon as we get off the phone, but I'm sure she understands the gravity of this weather and what it means." Karyn threw a coffee pod in her Keurig, then remembered the lack of electricity. She sighed, turned to her sister. "I could use your help at the lodge. When Clint gets here with the snowmobile, I'll come get you. Can you be ready?"

Leigh Ann agreed to her plan. "And I'll send Mark over to the church. Maybe he can take this cake. I mean, what else am I going to do with seven layers of strawberry champagne cake with cream cheese frosting?"

"Can't you freeze it?"

Leigh Ann inhaled sharply. "You're kidding, right? No one serves frozen cake at their wedding."

SOMETIME IN THE wee hours of that morning, the snow stake on Baldy disappeared. Its thirty-inch ruler, official arbiter of every storm, cleared daily at four p.m., barely held its head above mounting stacks of fresh snow. The light that illuminated it wasn't so lucky. Snow—some thirty inches overnight—blocked out the bulb. So, the storm, as seen safely indoors on Sun Valley's webcam, poured on, illumined only by the dim light of morning.

Over the past thirty-six hours, nearly four feet of snow had fallen on Bald Mountain, a record by anyone's estimation.

Joie sat with a steaming mug of coffee in her hands in front of the television.

"It was an interesting phenomenon—a double whammy," said the weather reporter. *"Two storms converged, with the bullseye right over central Idaho. We tend to get eight to twelve inches on a good storm. To see these sequences, dropping three to four feet? That's rare. For powder hounds, it's quite the gift. But for area residents who can't pull their cars out of their garages, not so much. Even the snow removal trucks are having a difficult time maneuvering the streets for clean-up. Electricity is off in much of the city. Water pipes are freezing. And, we have a few reports of roofs collapsing. No doubt, this storm will go down in the history books as 'Snowmageddon.'"*

Joie clicked the remote and turned off the broadcast.

Sure, there had been plenty of storm warnings, yet this situation had taken her by surprise. She'd never expected the weather to interrupt her wedding. While she'd struggled to embrace all the plans Leigh Ann had put in place, now that everything was canceled due to burgeoning snowdrifts, she couldn't help but feel terribly disappointed.

Joie twisted her engagement ring on her finger. She'd looked forward to wearing that gown—to exchanging vows with Clint. Today they would have become an official family—and it hurt to realize she'd wake tomorrow morning alone and still single.

It was as if she were being punished for all her past poor choices. Perhaps because, long ago, she popped the head off Leigh Ann's bridal Barbie and flushed it. Yes, fate had come back to bite her.

It certainly seemed like something, or someone, was against her. Maybe that wasn't how it worked, but it was difficult to believe anyone could be this unlucky.

By three o'clock in the afternoon, she and Hudson had been transported by sleigh and horses to Leigh Ann's house to wait. Karyn had moved in as well, after tiring of Leigh Ann's constant nagging that she shouldn't be staying in her house alone without electricity. "What if the storm dumps more snow?" she'd pointed out.

After a quick breakfast, her sisters had spent the better part of the day at the Sun Valley Lodge, dealing with broken pipes and lack of heat, which resulted in unhappy guests.

Her father and Clint remained over at the church. Early reports were that the roof collapse was isolated to the rear part of the building, the portion that housed the church offices. The chapel and the historic pews were salvaged. The roof was tarped and future damage remediated. A text from Clint told her they'd be wrapping up their efforts soon.

While a dedicated city staff had worked hard to clear the roads, many remained closed due to the heavy snow. The power company was hard at work to restore electricity but predicted it might be a couple of days before everything would be back to normal due to all the downed power lines.

Given all this, it would be difficult to predict when the wedding could be safely rescheduled. One thing for sure, it would not be today. Not without the church or the lodge or even electricity.

Once again, Joie felt herself slipping into a minor depression. What had she done to deserve this? Well, okay—the list of personal infractions was long. But, still.

She had just put Hudson down for a nap when she received another text from Clint.

"Hang tight. We're finishing up here, and then I'll come over to Leigh Ann's and get you. Roads are still a problem. They are having to haul snow out of the city limits. There's simply no place to pile it. I know you are disappointed our wedding plans were interrupted, but I've got everything under control. Just sit still—and don't worry."

That was easy for him to say. He didn't have to face all the disappointed townspeople, let alone another few weeks of Leigh Ann's harping about the added effort.

Joie grabbed a coat and stepped out onto Leigh Ann's front portico where she surveyed the frosty landscape. Up and down the street, the heavy blanket of snow was dappled with the shadows of the late-afternoon sun finally peeking through the clouds. She inhaled the fragrant, fresh air and tried to let go of the tension.

The important thing was that she would marry Clint— eventually. Just not tonight as planned.

24

A couple of hours passed. Hudson was sleeping well beyond his normal nap time. Likely all the morning commotion tuckered him out.

Joie wandered listlessly through Leigh Ann's house. She wasn't good at filling endless time with no one to talk to and nothing to do. She was tired of worrying the wedding situation to death. Internet reception was spotty at best, which made logging online and working not feasible. The only thing on television was weather reports, and Leigh Ann had very little in her house to do in the way of entertainment.

Bored out of her mind, Joie wandered over to the fireplace and stoked the fire. She added some wood from the basket Leigh Ann kept by the hearth, then she slipped onto the sofa and pulled Leigh Ann's afghan over her legs to ward off the chill. On the coffee table was one of those large, snotty books that people never actually read but kept on their tables to impress visitors.

She grabbed the heavy volume and lifted it onto her lap, opened the front cover to a photo essay on Japan and its culture. There were glossy photographs of delicate gardens with craggy mountains in the background. Others of pagodas and one of a woman wearing a colorful Jūnihitoe, a set of formal and highly complex kimono garments worn only by court-ladies in Japan.

At least she didn't have to get married in something like that.

She turned the page, and another image caught her eye—a beautiful piece of ceramic pottery. The piece looked to have been shattered and then mended with liquid gold.

Joie read on and learned that the bowl was representative of an ancient art form called Kintsugi: the art of precious scars.

This traditional Japanese art used a precious metal—liquid gold, liquid silver, or lacquer dusted with powdered gold—to bring together the pieces of a broken pottery item and at the same time enhance the breaks. The technique consisted of joining fragments and giving them a new, more refined aspect. Every repaired piece was unique, because of the randomness with which ceramics shatters and the irregular patterns formed that were enhanced with the use of the metals.

By repairing the broken ceramics, it was possible to give a new lease of life to pottery that became even more refined thanks to its "scars." The Japanese art of kintsugi taught that broken objects were not something to hide, but to display with pride.

The kintsugi technique suggested you shouldn't throw away broken objects. With proper care and restoration, the breakages became valuable—the essence of resilience.

Joie slowly closed the book and considered what she'd read.

In many ways, she was much like that piece of ceramic pottery. Her life was riddled with poor choices, bad mistakes, foolish antics that had pushed her life off-course in so many ways. In some amazing stroke of luck, a man named Clint Ladner had come into her life and had put her emotionally back together—had healed her broken scars. He saw her as a thing of beauty. As long as she lived, that fact would fill her with incredulous wonder.

She might not be able to marry him tonight because of circumstances she had no control over. No doubt, she would wait a lifetime, if she had to, in order to pledge herself to him— to become his wife. He was her betrothed, and she was his. That, indeed, was a thing of beauty. *Kintsugi.*

Smiling, she lifted from the sofa intending to go check on Hudson.

Suddenly, she heard a loud commotion outside.

Joie quickly moved to the front window and peered out. On the snow-covered lawn was her father's sleigh and horses with Clint holding the reins. He grinned and waved.

She quickly moved to the door, flung it open. "What's all this?"

He beamed. "Get ready. We have a wedding to go to."

"I—I don't understand. What are you saying?"

His face broke into an even wider grin. "You heard me. Go get Hudson. We're getting married."

Joie sat on a bale of hay on top of the sleigh, nestled up against Clint with little Hudson wrapped tightly in a blanket. The rhythmic jangle of the crossbar and whiffletrees swinging behind the horses was the only sound to break the silence as they made their way across the thick blanket of snow. Overhead, the dark night sky was punctuated by millions of tiny, bright stars—a clear indication the storm had passed.

"Where are we going?" Joie asked for the umpteenth time.

Clint snapped the reins and the horses picked up the pace, their clopping muffled by the snow as they continued down Dollar Road. "You'll see," he repeated.

They passed the Cottonwood Condominiums, made a

sharp left turn, and crossed onto an open area. The Sun Valley Stables came into view.

"We're heading for the stables?"

Clint only smiled.

The parking lot was empty. Clint pulled the reins back gently. "Eh-eh—that's it. That's it," he said as he pulled the horses to a stop. He motioned for her to wait as he jumped down and secured the team and led them inside a fenced off area. He then secured the horses by tethering them to a hitching post where fresh hay had been scattered and a trough of water awaited. Clint trudged back to the sleigh and held out his hand.

"Careful, the snow is deep in places."

She secured little Hudson against her hip and placed her free hand on Clint's shoulder, let him lift her down. "I'm confused, Clint. I thought you said we were getting married."

"We are," he told her as he took her hand and led her to the indoor arena—the same arena where she'd spent hours training Fresca. The same arena where they'd worked the rescue horses they'd picked up from the Fish and Game officials near Stanley all those many months ago.

It wasn't like Clint to be so mysterious. For the life of her, she could not figure out why they were here. She glanced around again at the empty parking lot, shook her head.

"Trust me," he said. "I'm always for you and never against you. You can trust that I will always have your back in every situation. That's how all this works."

They neared the big wooden sliding door that led into the arena. Little Hudson poked his tiny head from the blanket, smiled up at her like he was in on the secret. But, of course, he wasn't. How could he be?

Clint stopped, turned, and kissed her forehead. "I love you," he said. Then he flung the door open.

Only darkness inside.

Puzzled, Joie let Clint pull her inside.

Suddenly, what seemed like a million lights broke the darkness. Joie had to blink several times to adjust her vision.

They were here—all of them. And they were holding candles.

Her eyes flooded with tears.

Her dad stood by the door leading to the tack room, next to Leigh Ann and Mark. Karyn was there too. Colby stood not far from them with his arm around Nicole's shoulders. He waved.

Miss Trudy and Ruby waved too. As did Nash Billingsley and Lucy. Nash had traded his coffee apron for a coat jacket. Lucy wore a pretty skirt.

It seemed like the entire town was packed in that space, including Crusty and the guys, their faces beaming with excitement. Dick Cloudt held his candle up and hollered, "Fly high or go home, Chill." Chill was his nickname for her, a name he'd used in their skydiving days.

Joie wiped the tears. "I—I can't believe this." She looked over at Clint. "This is amazing."

He squeezed her hand. "I told you to trust me."

Her sisters rushed forward. "C'mon," Leigh Ann said. She took her arm and pulled. "We only have a few minutes to get you ready."

Her dad came forward and took little Hudson from her arms. It was then that she noticed Maddy Crane and the judge.

Her hand flew to her chest. "You—everything is perfect."

Leigh Ann pulled at her with a little more urgency. "Let's not hold up the party."

The tack room became her bridal room, lit by dozens of candles set inside mason jars and hanging from nails that had been driven in the wooden walls. On the hook that normally housed a bridle, her dress hung on a black velvet hanger.

Joie's lip quivered when she saw the gown.

She felt someone unbuttoning her shirt. Someone else

unhooked her belt buckle. In a short time, she was undressed and had slipped on the bridal gown.

Karyn pulled a brush through her hair before tucking her long tresses up in a messy bun. She used some sort of sticky hair gel and formed tiny curls hanging from her temples. Leigh Ann carefully placed tiny buds inside the folds.

In what seemed like no time, Cinderella was ready for her ball.

When the door to the tack room opened, Joie noted that a long red fabric runner had been placed on the dirt floor of the arena, lined by the flowers originally intended to deck the tables at the lodge. Mason jars with candles also bordered the fabric.

"Miss Trudy had this fabric in her attic," Leigh Ann whispered next to her ear.

She could barely breathe for the joy that filled her heart.

Her eyes followed the red path to where Clint stood in a suit next to Pastor John—waiting.

Suddenly, the sweetest melody filled the air—the sound of a violin. Crusty grinned as he pulled the bow across the strings of his instrument and Pachelbel's "Canon in D" sounded.

Joie couldn't believe what she was seeing—and hearing. This was amazing!

Her dad stepped alongside her, held out his elbow. "You ready, sweetheart?"

She nodded, slipped her hand inside the crook of his arm, gazed up at his face. Without warning, she was suddenly transported back to childhood, to when he would lift her and swing her around in the air with her shouting, "Again, Daddy. Again."

She swallowed hard, barely able to draw breath for the emotion welling inside her chest.

"Okay, let's go," he said.

She nodded.

They made their way down the aisle, trailed by her sisters,

past all the familiar faces filled with happiness at seeing her dream come true—of marrying a man who truly loved her.

At the end of the aisle, her father kissed her lightly on the forehead and handed her into Clint's extended hand. The music faded, and Pastor John smiled at them as her sisters stepped into place and flanked her side.

She leaned forward and whispered next to his ear. "Do you hear that? My heart pounding."

He grinned and whispered back, "My heart's pounding, too, just so you know." He squeezed her hand then nodded at Pastor John.

"Dearly beloved who are gathered, we are so delighted each of you is here to witness the marriage of Clint Ladner and Joie Abbott—a couple who have weathered quite the storm, in more ways than one." He smiled at them, before he proceeded. "It is my understanding that Clint and Joie would like to recite a few words before they complete their vows."

Clint took her hands in his, looked at her with those deep copper-colored eyes. He cleared his throat. "Joie Abbott, every part of me belongs to you. I love you. Not the love of butterflies and stomach knots—but more the blurring of self and the pure entanglement with another soul.

"I will choose you every day, giving you the best that I have and all my faithfulness. I will love you with my words and my actions, my decisions and my commitments. Your name will be safe on my lips. I will remind you how beautiful you are to me. I will encourage you, I will listen to you, and I will tell you what's on my heart. I will honor and love your child, Hudson, and will make him my own.

"I take you as you are now, tomorrow and for eternity to come, to be my wife. I vow to honor you and respect you, support you and encourage you. I will dream with you, celebrate with you, and walk beside you through whatever life brings. I'll laugh with you, comfort you during times of joy and times of sorrow and will love you unconditionally and whole-heartedly for the rest of my life. Joie, this is my unwavering promise."

Her lashes spiked with moisture, spilling over with happy tears.

He reached and tenderly wiped her cheek.

She could barely push the words she'd memorized from her tight throat. "Clint Ladner, I wasn't expecting you. In my wildest dreams, I had no idea we'd end up together. The single most extraordinary thing I've ever done with my life is fall in love with you. I've never been seen so completely—loved so passionately—protected so fiercely. In your eyes, I see my home. I see eternity. No matter what may come our way, I promise I will always follow you, no matter where that leads. I will honor you with my life and cherish you until I take my last breath. I love you."

They completed their vows and Pastor John's face broke into a pleased grin. "I now pronounce you husband and wife. You may now kiss the bride."

Clint obliged, pressed a tender kiss onto her lips. She couldn't help but weep with joy.

She was no longer shattered by her insecurity, her choices, and missteps. She was Mrs. Clint Ladner—a woman sweetly broken, wholly surrendered to a man who loved her—a man she could trust with her entire heart. Especially in the storms of life.

25

Leigh Ann, Karyn, and Joie stood on their father's porch. In the yard, Clint patiently waited in his pickup loaded with luggage.

"You have a good time in Hawaii. And don't worry about Hudson," Leigh Ann told her as she pulled her into a side hug. "Uncle Mark and Aunt Leigh Ann will take excellent care of him."

Joie shook the concern from her face, kissed the top of her son's downy hair. "I know you will."

Karyn stepped forward, grabbed her little sister, and hugged her fiercely. "I'm so proud of you, Joie." Her eyes shone with tears.

Joie grinned. "I'm proud of you too. It takes a lot of courage to change course in life. I'm so excited for your upcoming move.

Karyn nodded, pulled her little sister in tighter before letting her go.

Clint honked. He hung out the open window. "Joie, c'mon. If we don't get on the road, we're going to miss our flight."

She nodded, held onto one of each of her sisters' hands several seconds before letting go. "Okay, I'm coming."

She turned and ran for the pickup, taking care not to slip on the icy path. She climbed inside, shut the pickup door, and waved. "See you in a week," she hollered back at them.

They waved wildly. "Have a good time," they called out as Clint started the engine and slowly pulled away, and maneuvered down the lane.

Leigh Ann patted little Hudson's back. "We'll have our own little luau right here, won't we, buddy?" Her face turned solemn. "You know, I'm not happy about all these goodbyes—even if they are temporary."

Karyn gave her shoulders a hug. "I know. But I've already booked you a ticket to fly out to California and help me set up the restaurant. I can't do it alone, you know."

Leigh Ann gently rocked back and forth, still patting Hudson. "Jon is going to have a cow with us both gone. He didn't exactly take the news of your resignation all that well."

"I'm leaving the lodge in good hands." Karyn moved to the table next to an empty rocking chair, grabbed the mug of coffee sitting there. "Have you told him the news about Happenings?"

"Yes, and I still can't believe Croslyn Merritt was so impressed with Joie's wedding that she offered me a spot as a contributing editor on her blog. Between that and being the permanent hospitality director for the Sun Valley Lodge, I'll barely have time to miss you." She playfully nudged Karyn's shoulder with her own." Despite the comment, her eyes painted a different story.

"I'm going to miss you terribly," Karyn admitted. "It was easy to think about such a dramatic move in the abstract. But not living near you, Joie, and Dad is going to be a huge adjustment."

Leigh Ann waved her off. "Don't start. I've cried enough about it." She peeked inside the blanket at her nephew. "Well, what do you say, Champ? You ready to get going?" She looked at Karyn. "He has been pretty fussy today. Must be all the excitement. What he needs is some quiet and a little structure."

A tiny smile nipped at the corner of Karyn's mouth. She drew her mug up and took a sip. "Yeah, you're probably right."

"Oh, I know I'm right. And, by the way, I packed up some canned tomatoes to take to California with you. They may grow fabulous grapes out there in the Sunshine State, but their tomatoes can't compete with Idaho."

Karyn threw back her head and laughed. "No, of course not."

Karyn followed Leigh Ann to her car, where she put Hudson in his car seat. When he was securely fastened in, she turned and gave Karyn a brief hug before heading for the driver side door. "So, I'll be there in the morning to help you finish packing," she said over the top of the car. "And Mark wants to look over the closing papers before you sign."

Karyn nodded. "Okay. That's great."

She walked back onto the porch, stood, and watched as her sister put her SUV in four-wheel drive and pulled away.

Then, she was alone.

She'd certainly come a long way since that day at the Hemingway Memorial—the day she couldn't face letting Dean go. She'd weathered a lot since then. Falling in love again, and then being forced into letting go. Taking a risk and working as the hospitality director for the Sun Valley Lodge. Somehow, she'd loosened her grip on the need to please everyone else and had decided to focus on what would make her happy. She had a bright future to look forward to, and that was what she would focus on now.

Leigh Ann would be fine without her there, she knew. Colby and Nicole would have babies soon, and Leigh Ann would smother her grandbabies with as much love as she had with all her family. The lodge was left in capable hands with her at the helm, and Karyn looked forward to reading Leigh Ann's weekly blog posts on the Happenings website.

Joie had a bright future ahead as well. She was no longer the wayward young girl who took risky chances. Her younger sister had settled down. She was a wife and mother, and now seemed to fit in her skin finally.

Her law practice was thriving. She and Clint would move into their new home and raise little Hudson, and hopefully more babies, out here on their father's ranch.

Karyn would certainly miss her dad. With any luck, she'd be able to talk him into taking a real vacation and visiting her in California. She might even get him into one of those fancy mud baths.

Karyn took a deep breath and looked out over the horizon, trying to memorize every inch of the ranch she'd grown up on. In a few weeks, she'd be miles away. It wouldn't be easy to leave this place, say goodbye to those who held her heart.

But she knew this—she would carry it all with her wherever she went. Most especially, her sisters.

AFTERWORD

Hey, everybody—Miss Trudy here. Kellie and I are so glad you joined us for another story in the Sun Valley series. I have to ask, wasn't this story romantic? That wedding had me in tears, girls. Simply in tears!

Like her sisters (and likely all of you) I was surprised to learn Karyn is moving to California. But word on the street (and I have it from very good sources) Kellie plans to kick-off another series set in the Napa Valley area in California. So, this won't be the last you'll see of these Karyn and her sisters.

Even better news, Kellie has been working hard on a completely new series that will be debuting early in 2020. This new series will be set in one of her favorite places—the Oregon coast. So, scoot on over to her website and sign up for her newsletter so you won't miss out on new release notices.

And don't forget to check out the Love on Vacation stories, also set in Sun Valley. These shorter length romances are packed with tales of dating and mating, love and marriage and promise to keep your funny bone on high alert. You'll also see a few characters you will recognize from the Sun Valley series show up on occasion.

Well, I've got to scoot. But we'll see each other soon, I hope!
~Miss Trudy

ABOUT THE AUTHOR

Kellie Coates Gilbert has won readers' hearts with her compelling and highly emotional stories about women and the relationships that define their lives. A former legal investigator, she is especially known for keeping readers turning pages and creating nuanced characters who seem real.

In addition to garnering hundreds of five-star reviews, Kellie has been described by RT Book Reviews as a "deft, crisp story-teller." Her books were featured as Barnes & Noble Top Shelf Picks and were included on Library Journal's Best Book List.

Born and raised near Sun Valley, Idaho, Kellie now lives with her husband of over thirty-five years in Dallas, where she spends most days by her pool drinking sweet tea and writing the stories of her heart.

www.kelliecoatesgilbert.com

ALSO BY KELLIE COATES GILBERT

Mother of Pearl

Sisters (Sun Valley Series Book 1)

Heartbeats (Sun Valley Series Book 2)

Changes (Sun Valley Series Book 3)

Promises (Sun Valley Series Book 4)

Otherwise Engaged – a Love on Vacation Story

All Fore Love – a Love on Vacation Story

A Woman of Fortune - Texas Gold Book 1

Where Rivers Part - Texas Gold Book 2

A Reason to Stay - Texas Gold Book 3

What Matters Most - Texas Gold Book 4

More information and purchase links can be found at:

www.kelliecoatesgilbert.com

SNEAK PEEK - A WOMAN OF FORTUNE

Download your copy of this book for FREE at your favorite retailer! Or, go to Kellie's website:

www.kelliecoatesgilbert.com

~~~

Until today, Claire Massey had never been inside the walls of a federal prison.

She'd taken French cooking lessons in Paris, photographed the aurora borealis, and even dined with a president and his wife. But never in her wildest imagination could she have contemplated herself doing this.

She fingered the fine-grain leather bag in her lap as the car slowly moved through heavy metal gates and past the guard tower that strangely resembled a childhood fort.

"You okay, Mom?"

She startled at her son's voice. "What? Uh, yes, I'm fine." Her hand plunged inside her purse for her Dolce & Gabbana sunglasses.

Max took a deep breath. "You don't have to do this, you know."

Claire nodded, keeping her eyes averted from the razor wire that cut a line across the horizon. She slipped the glasses on, glad for the barrier between her budding tears and the harsh Texas sun reflecting off the building looming ahead.

She swallowed. Hard. This was no time to lose it.

After pulling one hand from the steering wheel, her son slipped his palm over her trembling fingers. "Please, Mom, let me go in with you."

She shook her head. "No, this is something I need to do. Alone."

Max circled the parking lot twice before finding an empty spot. He pulled the car between a pickup with wheels the size of her car door and a battered green sedan that had definitely seen better days. From its rearview mirror hung a rosary and a pair of red lace panties, the kind you might see on a Victoria's Secret model.

Her son cut the engine.

Claire took a deep breath. "I don't know how long this will take."

Something in Max's eyes dimmed. He scratched at his beard stubble. "I'll be here."

The line at the front door extended several hundred yards. Claire moved with caution into place at the end, behind a heavy woman clothed in a stained housedress and slipper-like shoes that dug deeply into swollen flesh.

She shifted uncomfortably in her own wedge pumps, aware she'd made a questionable shoe choice. Why hadn't she thought to wear tennis shoes? The woman she'd talked to on the telephone yesterday warned Saturday was their heaviest day for visitors, cautioning the line would be like this.

Forty minutes passed before Claire reached the front-entry door and stepped into the large, old brick building and out of the baking sun, the inside air a welcome respite from the heat emanating from the concrete she'd been standing on. Despite the cooler temperature, sweat formed on her scalp. The heat perhaps? Or maybe nerves. She couldn't tell.

From somewhere in the line behind her, a young girl shushed her squalling infant. Claire couldn't help but think this was no place for a baby. But then again, would any of them be here if given a better option?

A woman officer dressed in a blue shirt, damp at the underarms, stepped forward. "I'll need your driver's license." She thrust a clipboard at Claire. "Sign at the designated spot and put the time next to your name." She tilted her head toward a large clock on the opposite wall. "And place your belongings in the basket."

Claire looked up. "My belongings?"

The woman sighed. "Rings, watch. You can't take nothing in with you."

"But my purse—"

"Nothing," she repeated.

Claire swallowed and did as she was told. When finished, she held up the basket to the officer.

The woman pointed to a wall lined with lockers and handed Claire a key. "Over there."

As soon as she stored her belongings, she glanced around, confused about where to go next. An older black lady with white hair gave her a toothy smile and pointed toward a metal door with a sign posted above that read "Visitors Holding Room."

Claire gave her a token nod of gratitude and followed a crowd of people moving in that direction. After passing through the metal detector, she was patted down by another female officer, who smelled of cigarettes and maple syrup. "Wait over there," the woman said, pointing to metal chairs lined up against a pea-green wall in bad need of paint.

She nodded and scanned for an empty chair, then sat to wait.

A man moved past, mopping the floor. His shoes made a slight squeaky sound every time he sludged forward, slowly pulling the dirty-looking mop across the speckled linoleum floor.

Claire looked away, focusing instead on a fake philodendron wedged in the corner, a few feet away from a drinking fountain hanging from the wall. Anything to quiet the voices in her head. Especially Jana Rae's.

"What are you? Ten shades of stupid?" her friend had asked over the phone.

"Look, this is something I need to do," Claire explained.

"Claire, listen to me. This crazy idea is going to put you square on the wrong end of an intervention. You know what I mean? Haven't you been through enough already?"

That was one thing Claire loved about Jana Rae. Few people could truly be counted on in life. Her crazy friend with blazing red hair and a mouth snappy as a bullwhip had always been in her corner of the arena. Even now.

Claire leaned her head back against the cold, hard wall of the holding room, keeping her eyes closed so she wouldn't have to see countless young girls waiting to see their baby daddies. The sight was far too depressing. But then, she wasn't so different. A female who had stood by her man and looked the other way, failing to see things as they really were.

Funny how she'd always known the grass was green—but never needed to know how or why.

She gnawed on her bottom lip, a habit she'd taken up as of late.

"Claire Massey?"

The booming voice caused her to startle. Claire glanced about the room as if there might be another woman with that name. "Me?" she asked.

The woman officer with the clipboard heaved a sigh laced with boredom. "Your name Massey?"

She nodded and stood. She followed the officer through the door and down a long hallway with windowless walls the color of the dried mud lining the pond out at Legacy Ranch, the one she'd gazed out at each morning while sitting in the breakfast nook.

The woman led her through a heavy metal door into a room less than half the size of her bathroom at home. Granted, the bathroom had been much larger than most, but this space felt cramped nonetheless.

A barrier cut the room in half, the upper portion made of glass grimy with handprints. The scene was straight out of a television episode of *CSI*.

Claire turned to thank the officer, but she was now alone. Nervous, she slid into the empty chair on her side of the barrier.

And waited.

Claire told herself to breathe. Her heart pounded wildly, and by the time the door on the other side of the barrier creaked open, every nerve fiber in her body was charged. It would take next to nothing to spark tears.

She trained her eyes on the doorway and vowed not to cry. Not here.

Then he entered, appearing older, more tired than the last time she'd seen him. Perhaps resigned to his circumstances. But he still looked at her with the same eyes—the ones she'd gazed into that night all those years ago at the Burger Hut. And so many times since.

Tuck quickly moved to the window and took his seat. With a guard standing nearby, he placed his shackled palm against the glass and mouthed, "I love you."

Claire blinked several times before picking up the telephone receiver and motioning for him to do the same.

He scrambled for the phone at his side, as though it were a line to the life he'd left behind . . . to her. He quickly nestled the black handset against his ear. \

"Claire." He said her name with a kind of reverence, a tone you'd use with someone you cherished.

Claire swallowed against the dryness of her throat. She looked into her husband's eyes and steeled herself.

"I want a divorce."

Download your copy of this book for FREE at your favorite retailer! Or, go to Kellie's website:

www.kelliecoatesgilbert.com

SNEAK PEEK - MOTHER OF PEARL

"Where's Graeber?"

I freeze. Guess it was only a matter of time before Coach Warren came gunning for me. I toss my coffee in the sink, listening while Bill Miller, the pudgy biology teacher who always smells of formaldehyde, rats me out. "Barrie? I just saw her heading for the teachers' lounge."

"Graeber," the coach barks as he storms through the doorway. "What's the deal with you pulling Dennis Cutler off the team right before our big game?"

Okay, here goes. I muster everything I've been taught about effective communication and look Coach Warren directly in those deep blue eyes. No way is he going to bully me. "I did not pull the Cutler boy. I simply asked Sharon to enforce what we all agreed upon last spring. His academic improvement plan requires him to attend the special tutoring sessions I put in place. As it stands now, he's not going to pass his core subjects and graduate. I already went to bat for him once, based on a promise he'd work hard this year."

Coach Warren shakes his head. "But—"

"But nothing. Sleeping through his classes and skipping

tutoring sessions is not acceptable. I'm sorry, I really am. But we both know if Dennis is not on target to graduate, he's ineligible to play. Simple as that."

When I tell people I'm a school guidance counselor, they think it means I spend hours helping students fill out college application and FAFSA forms. And that's true. But my job is so much more. I'm here to advocate for my students, to look out for their best interests. Sometimes that means protecting them from a coach who has yet to understand that the one with the most trophies can still wind up a loser.

Don't get me wrong. I have nothing against a good football game. But why must education always take a back seat to sports? Truth is, in this town football reigns. Academics are often abandoned and left to drift to shore while the athletic program leans back, clipping along like a Kennedy on a sailboat.

Warren pulls his arms tighter across the chest of a jacket that reads *Sawtooth High Cougars.* "So, let me get this straight. You're going to let down a whole team, the entire town of Falcon, Idaho for that matter . . . what, so you can make a point?"

I huff. "That is the point. When Dennis failed to do his part and study, he's the one who let his team down." I feel myself gaining emotional steam. "And what does it say if we let Dennis flunk out? Will that prepare him for his future?" Satisfied I'd made my point, I smugly climb down from my imaginary soapbox.

Coach Warren unfolds his arms and leans forward. With a lowered voice he speaks, pausing between each word for emphasis. "I don't give a rat's tail about how nice little Dennis's future is. That's your job. Mine is to win football games."

Before I can respond, several teachers enter the lounge. Coach Warren instantly plants a smile on his face and works the room like a politician, assuring everyone that yes indeed, the Cougars will put the Vikings back on the bus after the game this afternoon with their heads hanging low. He glances back at me. Those striking blue eyes narrow to drive his point home.

"Count on it," he says.

Nobody wants to admit this, but often adults don't understand how hard life is for teenagers these days. In this pressure-cooker life, young people need someone they can trust, someone who will encourage them to work hard so they can accomplish their dreams.

That's where I come in.

I head for my counseling office, a tight little room lined with bookshelves filled with college catalogs and FAFSA publications. Sliding into the chair behind my badly marred walnut desk, I pull a scheduling book from the drawer and assess what the rest of my morning holds.

A knock at the door alerts me to my first appointment—Cade Walton, a kid whose single mom is working two jobs so he can attend college next fall. I motion him in and have him take a seat. Then, lifting his file from the stack on my desk, I begin my work for the day.

By four o'clock, I've finished my student interviews and move to grab my coat and gloves. Today is the only afternoon football game of the season and I'm anxious to join the cheering crowd I hear outside my window.

Moving quickly I juggle my purse and coat while trying to lock my office door.

"Mrs. Graeber?"

I turn to find Emily Jorgensen, a rather high-strung girl who comes from a family of known achievers.

"Hey, Emily. What can I do for you?"

Emily bursts into tears.

I muffle a sigh, unlock my door and invite her into my office. I hand the distraught girl a tissue and she plops down in the chair at the side of my desk, apparently oblivious to the fact nearly every other student from Sawtooth High School is currently out at the football field.

My eyes glance at the wall clock. Pearl's dance team is performing during halftime, and I don't want to miss seeing my daughter execute the moves she's been practicing all week.

"Okay, sweetie, why the tears?"

"It's just that Mr. Baxter won't relent on my grade in English comp, and if I don't score at least a ninety-seven, my chance to get accepted to Harvard will be ruined."

I lean closer, slightly amused at her melodrama but silently wishing all students I counsel cared this much about their academic careers. "Emily, I know you worry." I look her directly in the eye to make sure she feels validated. "But, you are an excellent student. A single grade on one paper this early in your senior year won't impact your university plans. I promise. Besides, a ninety-five is still impressive."

The plain looking girl, who has yet to come out of her shell and even wear makeup, looks unconvinced.

After sneaking another look at the clock, I opt for a different approach. "But tell you what, I'll talk to Mr. Baxter and see what extra credit opportunities he'll be offering this semester." Mindful of the no touching rule imposed on educators these days, I still stand and give her a brief hug. "In the meantime, focus on doing your best. That's really all you can do."

The teary-eyed girl nods and moves for the door. "Thanks, Mrs. Graeber. I really appreciate it." She gives me a little wave as she leaves.

After cramming her file in my drawer, I gather my things for a second time and head out to the big game.

Stepping into crisp fall air, I hurry past lines of parked cars toward the sound of band drums and referee whistles. Slowing, I flash my staff badge at the tired looking security guard at the gate before continuing toward the stands. My eyes pan the crowd until I finally locate Joe and Connie Anderson and my son, Aaron. I wave and make my way up the bleachers.

"Where've you been?" Connie scoots over, making room for me.

I roll my eyes. "Don't ask."

Connie's expression turns sympathetic. "Well, we're about to finish second quarter."

My son greets me without pulling his gaze from the field. "Hey, Mom."

"Hi, sweetheart." Glancing around to see if I can spot Pearl, I move to give my son a hug before I remember my eleven-year-old hates any public display of affection.

I turn to Connie's husband. "Hey there, Joe."

Joe Anderson is one of Steve's closest buddies. They go way back, football teammates from when they attended Sawtooth years ago.

No one loves football more than Joe. Despite his respected position on the school board, he's been known to yell like a banshee when the Cougars' score falls behind. I dip my hand in his container of popcorn, painfully aware I should never have skipped lunch today. "Where's Steve?"

Joe nervously scans the field. "No sign of him yet."

"I'm not surprised," I eye his popcorn but decide it'd be rude to grab another handful. Instead, I check my phone for messages. "My husband is always running late these days. If he doesn't quit burning the candle at both ends, he's going to wind up with a heart attack before he turns forty."

The scoreboard at the south end of the field flashes twenty-one to twenty. Too close for comfort. Barely in our favor. Joe tells me we'd run the ball well so far, but the Vikings' place kicker had been hot. Now, with just a minute left in the second quarter, they'd punched up the grass into field goal range. Lowering my gaze to the forty-yard line, I breeze past the action to the sidelines.

"Oh look, there's Pearl." Beaming, I pull up my cell phone and shoot a photo. I watch as she waves at number thirty-two as he jogs back to the sidelines from the line of scrimmage.

Pearl has been going out with Craig Ellison, the team's quarterback, for a little over a year. Together, they look like the Ken and Barbie dolls I played with growing up. At times, I worry they might be getting a bit too close. She has a whole lifetime ahead of her, and I certainly don't want her duplicating my mistakes.

I'd worry a lot more if she wasn't with a boy like Craig. He's a polite kid from a good family. When Pearl was in junior high, I co-chaired a school carnival with his mom.

Back at the field's edge, Coach Warren and his assistant huddle with the defense, barking out orders. With a slap on the back of number forty-two, he launches the players out on the field.

"C'mon! Hold the line!" Aaron screams.

I join the rest of the crowd already on their feet when the Vikings' quarterback takes the snap and drops into the pocket. He scans for an open receiver as he pats the ball once. Twice. Then he whips the ball past his ear and a perfect spiral soars forty yards into the straining hands of the Vikings' tight end. He cradles the ball tight and sprints for the goal line.

"STOP HIM!" the diminutive woman in front of us belches out, causing more than a few of us to look at her in surprise.

The crowd across the field explodes into cheers. I snap my head back to the action just in time to watch the Viking receiver cross the goal line and slam the ball on the end zone grass. A routine extra point a minute later cements their lead at halftime.

Joe curses and I reach for my phone, thinking I'll text Steve to see if he's going to make it in time for Pearl's halftime show.

"Mom, can I have some money for popcorn?" Aaron holds his hand outstretched.

"What happened to the twenty I gave you yesterday?"

He explains in detail, reminding me buying his vintage Joe Namath card cleaned him out. I hand him my wallet. "Put it back in my purse. And only take a twenty."

He follows my directions, then starts down the bleachers. "And get me some," I add.

Connie gives me a nudge. "Barrie, the dance team's taking the field. Hey, there's Pearl." She points.

I let my cell phone drop back into my purse and crane my neck around the tall guy in front of me. Nobody gets between me and the half-time show.

My daughter takes her place in the formation with the rest of the group at the edge of the field. She's been practicing for this routine every night this week, working hard to master the complicated moves.

On the field, girls in gold-colored glittery tops and short black skirts march in precision formations to the Star Wars theme song. My daughter snaps her head left in unison with twenty other girls from her spot, third from the end.

When the dance team finishes their final number, uniformed band members follow the girls off the field, playing the last strains of a snappy march. I am applauding with the rest of the crowd, when Steve juggles his way past the Andersons and moves in next to me on the bleachers. "Sorry I'm late." He kisses my cheek. "What'd I miss?"

Joe shakes his head. "The Vikings just crept ahead. I hate to say this, but I hope Coach cleans clock at halftime. That Baker kid especially."

"Honey—" Connie looks at her husband with disbelief.

"How can you say that? You know Vince Baker's mother is battling cancer. Cut the poor kid some slack."

Brushing his hand across his shaved head, Joe continues looking out at the field. "Well, another wrong move and we won't even have a chance at playoffs."

Connie rolls her eyes, leans over and says in a low voice, "I swear, he'd sell his grandmother to win a football game." Steve's eyes lock with mine and we share a smile.

Aaron climbs back up in the stands, his hands juggling a hotdog, two bags of popcorn and cola. "Hey, Dad." He hands one of the popcorns to me.

"Hi, Scoot." Steve ruffles our son's hair. A flicker of guilt crosses my husband's face as he leans over to me. "So, did I miss Pearl's halftime routine?"

"Afraid so, honey." I smile and offer him some popcorn. "But don't worry, she'll understand. I almost missed her routine myself because of a meeting with a student."

"I thought you didn't have any afternoon appointments?"

I lean toward him and lower my voice. "A student showed up in tears."

Steve nods. "Ahh."

I stretch my hand out toward Aaron. "Hey, where's my change?"

My son grins and juggles his drink while he reaches in his back pocket. I relent and tell him he can keep the money if he'll help me rake the leaves tomorrow His face brightens. "Sure!"

Minutes later the players take the field and the third quarter begins.

A sense of palpable excitement throbs in the bleachers as the Vikings kick off to the Cougars' line of receivers. I find myself holding my breath as the Cutler kid lines himself up with the soaring ball. Wait—?

I shade my eyes for a better look. "Steve, is that Dennis Cutler out there?"

"Yeah, why?"

A wave of frustration hits me like a tsunami. Looks like Mr. GQ Coach got his way after all. No telling what strings he'd pulled this time.

I shake my head. "Long story." Miffed, I tell myself that Michael Warren may have won for now, but I'll make sure this issue is revisited.

On the field, Dennis catches the ball and races down the field, advancing thirty yards before a Viking slips past one of our blockers and tackles him to the ground. Joe and Steve high-five each other. The ref blows his whistle and Pearl's boyfriend, Craig, jogs out to the field and gathers the team in a huddle. Seconds later, they break and move to the line of scrimmage.

My attention diverts to our daughter, gathered with her friends on the edge of the field. Her laughter fills my heart with joy.

It's true. A mother loves all her children the same. But I have to admit I feel especially connected to my firstborn. Maybe because for the first four years of her life, it was just the two of us.

Steve leans over and whispers in my ear—"Where're you at?"—which is his way of telling me he notices I've been deep in thought and not plugged in to the game. I smile and weave my fingers in his, enjoying the feel of his calloused palms against my own.

Just before the game ends, our receiver sprints into the end zone. The extra point a minute later hands us our victory.

Joe lets out a whoop followed by a rather colorful expletive. Connie slaps his arm. "Watch it," she nods toward Aaron. "We have young ears nearby."

"That Craig sure has an arm," Steve says, his face beaming as if Pearl's boyfriend were his own son. And he might as well be, for the amount of time he spends in our home.

After a few parents in the stands mutter, "*great game,*" and *"knew Coach Warren would pull off another one,"* I gather my things and trundle down the bleachers with the Andersons and Steve. Aaron trails close behind.

We make our way out to the parking lot before Joe turns to Steve. "The Kiwanis are holding a reception for the coach Tuesday night. You guys going?" Holding my breath, I wait for Steve's reply.

"Naw, can't. Got a meeting with my new business partner and it'll likely run into the evening."

At least I've been spared *that* misery. The last thing I want to do is join a mob of Coach Warren worshipers.

We wave our goodbyes to the Andersons, agreeing to try to get together for dinner soon, when Pearl rushes up, breathless. "Hey, Mom. Craig isn't going to be able to take me home. Something about a team meeting with the Coach. He said he'd pick me up later, so can I catch a ride with you?" Without waiting for a reply, she turns to Steve, looping her arm in his. "So Dad, what did you think of my routine?"

Coming to Steve's rescue, I jump into the conversation. "We're both very proud of how you did, sweetie." Pearl grins and says she'll gather her things and meet me at the car.

"I owe you one," Steve tells me as soon as Aaron is several steps ahead and out of earshot.

"Only one?" I tease. "Oh, and you'll need to pick up chicken on the way home because I don't have anything thawed."

"Again?" A grin crosses his face and his hand playfully slaps my behind. Laughing, he hurries to catch up with Aaron. He places his arm around our son's shoulder and I listen to their fading discussion about which team the Cougs will be matched up with in the playoffs.

Pearl joins me at the car a few minutes later. She's changed out of her dance uniform into a cute pair of jeans and a light yellow sweater that sets off her blue eyes. No longer pulled back in a ponytail, her lengthy blonde curls fall over her shoulders. I look at her and wonder if she has any idea how beautiful she is.

She smiles. "What are you looking at, Mom?"

"You, sweetheart."

She waves me off. "What did you think of the routine?"

Before I can respond, she goes on to tell me she thinks she missed a step, in the third set of ten count, but hopes no one noticed. I assure her she looked perfect out there.

"Dad didn't get there in time, did he?"

The question catches me a bit off guard. "Well, no honey. But he wanted to. Traffic just held him up." I watch her face in order to gauge her thoughts, something that is progressively more difficult as she gets older.

She shrugs and smiles. "Oh, I know. I'm not making a big deal of it, I just kinda need you to understand you don't have to treat me like I'm gonna break over something like that."

I open my mouth to interrupt, but she goes on.

"Mom, I think I found the perfect shoes to match the dress we bought for homecoming."

"Oh? How much?"

"I know the dress cost a lot, but these shoes are perfect. So, I've already arranged to babysit for Mrs. Emberly next weekend.

I nod, wondering when my daughter became so responsible. I'm tempted to give myself a pat on the back, but raising kids is a day-to-day task. One I wouldn't trade for the world.

We chat while I drive. She tells me about her trig class and about the upcoming play she might try out for in drama, about the low-lights she'd like to have in her hair and says she's out of nail polish remover, could I pick her up some tomorrow.

"Mom, Callie heard that Craig and I have a good chance of being voted King and Queen at the Homecoming Dance."

"Honey, that's wonderful." I smile and check the rearview mirror, before changing lanes.

Pearl grabs a tissue from the compartment on the dash and spits her gum into it, wadding the Kleenex into a tight ball. "And the decorations are really going to be over the top. Our committee agreed nothing cutesy this year. So, Coach suggested we go with a casino theme."

"The coach? What's he doing advising the Homecoming Dance committee?"

"He offered. Besides, he has the *best* ideas. Way better than Mrs. Franklin's. Last year she pushed for that awful hoedown theme. No one wants to sit on a bale of straw while dressed in a gown."

I frown. "But, I'm not sure a Vegas-like theme is appropriate for—"

Suddenly, her head darts to the window. "Mom, slow down."

"What?"

"Turn around, quick." "Pearl—"

"Mom, please—" she pleads. "Just turn around. Hurry."

I grip the wheel and check my mirrors. Finding the way clear, I whip my Acura around then glance back in Pearl's direction. "What's going on?"

She points at a pickup parked near the back of the Texas Roadhouse restaurant. "There."

I slow the car and my eyes follow where she points to a guy letting a girl out of his truck. *Craig's* truck. He bends and kisses —Callie.

My eyes dart back to Pearl. She sees as well. With tears pooling, she barks, "Go! Don't let them see us."

I nod and quickly pull away. "Oh, honey . . ."

She holds her hand up. "Mom, stop. Don't say anything. Not now."

I watch helplessly while my daughter's face crumbles and tears roll down her cheeks. I take a frail breath, wanting desperately to find the right words.

When she was little and fell off her bike, I knew how to bandage a scraped knee. And as her heart filled with disappointment in junior high when the principal awarded the coveted science fair prize to someone else, I knew how to salve her hurt feelings. But this time, a still voice deep inside my head warns me to do as she asked and remain quiet. At least for now.

Moms are supposed to run interference for their children, protect them from the hard things in life. Perhaps for the first time, I understand mothers can't fix all things.

I press my foot on the accelerator and focus on the road ahead, silently driving my daughter and her broken heart home.

Order your copy today at your favorite retailer, or visit Kellie's website:

www.kelliecoatesgilbert.com

SNEAK PEEK - WHERE RIVERS PART

Conference hotels all look the same.

This is what Juliet Ryan thought as she stepped into the lobby of the Renaissance Marriott Convention Center, with its enormous floral arrangements and lengthy granite-topped counter lined with check-in clerks and their pasted smiles.

Even though she'd given up the secret vice months ago, Juliet found herself wanting a cigarette. Especially today, when the need to calm her nerves with a few quick puffs tugged at her like a leash.

She mentally shook off the craving and gave herself a pep talk. She had no reason to feel this anxious. Not really.

Then why was she letting him back in her head?

In quality control circles, the North American Food Safety Symposium (NAFSS) was the pinnacle in a very high stack of conferences held across the nation each year. Even her father would have to admit her inclusion signaled a grand recognition among her peers that she'd finally made it. This conference featured only the elite candidates in the food safety field, and she was one of them. She had every reason to feel confident.

After fishing a schedule from the leather attaché hanging

from her shoulder, she quickly located the Grand Ballroom on the map and made her way down a long hall in that direction. . Midway, she stopped to check her lipstick in a mirror that reflected an image of exactly what she hoped to portray—an educated, accomplished young woman who had earned the respect of her colleagues, not an easy feat in a field overrun with testosterone and gray hair.

Her spot on the dais was third from the end on a row of tables seating nine—not exactly the first order of prestige, but nonetheless a position of some cachet. After her presentation today, no doubt she'd cement a spot closer to the head of the table, even if she were the only woman presenter again next year.

On stage, Dr. Keller Thatcher, director of NAFSS, read off the impressive credentials of each of the panel members, while an audience of bobbleheads nodded their collective approval.

The first to take the podium was Leonard Paternoster, a plaintiffs' attorney who had carefully cultivated his notoriety after winning several highly publicized landmark awards—all delineated in the brochure Juliet nervously folded in her hands.

Mr. Paternoster gripped the podium. "Good morning, everyone. I am an attorney specializing in foodborne illness cases. Before I go any further, I need to disclose that I am here for one reason alone—and that is to help you put me out of business."

Juliet listened to the spiel she'd heard many times before, knowing the somber-faced attorney had been positioned to go first for good reason. The threat of a lawsuit always made people in the food industry sit up and pay attention. No one wanted another deadly restaurant outbreak like the Jack in the Box situation in the nineties.

She'd been in junior high when a silver-haired talk show personality named Phil Donahue interviewed those affected by the outbreak. Juliet's father wanted to take credit for her career choice, but really, the moment Juliet knew she wanted to spend her professional life pursuing food safety was triggered by that television program and the look in Vicki Detwiler's eyes as she described how her seventeen-month-old son tested positive for E. coli, and his agonizing last hours.

Of course, her career choice came with a few drawbacks. A person trained to ensure safety and wholesomeness of food products was rarely at the top of any dinner party guest list. She also hadn't counted on the bleak disinterest in men's eyes when they discovered how many hours she devoted to pathogens and coliforms.

Still, for all the disadvantages, Juliet loved her profession. Her work mattered.

She held on to this satisfying thought as she took her turn at the podium.

"Good morning. My name is Dr. Juliet Ryan, quality assurance director for Larimar Springs Corporation. I'm here to bring an added perspective to what my esteemed colleagues have shared this morning, and look at these issues from inside the walls of the food producer." Duplicating her father's calculated method for creating impact, she leaned forward ever so slightly and made eye contact with the audience. "We are on the front line, charged with keeping America's food products safe."

Over the next hour, Juliet communicated her carefully memorized points, all constructed to balance the often skewed belief that food corporations only thought in terms of the financial bottom line, then moved to her closing statements.

"Companies across America are using the most sophisticated scientific techniques available to refine the processes used to kill pathogens." She paused for emphasis, appreciating that every eye was focused on her and what she had to say. Her message had hit its mark with the distinguished audience. This was her moment in the spotlight, and she'd satisfactorily shone.

Relieved, she took a deep breath and concluded, "Consumer health and safety are at the very core of what we do every day, and because of the collective efforts of dedicated food scientists and quality assurance directors in companies across America, outbreaks are now rare, with fewer reported each year than ever before." She let her lips part in a wide smile, showing off gleaming (and costly) white teeth. "Thank you."

Juliet waited until the applause faded before extending appreciation to the directors of the symposium for inviting her to speak. She straightened her notes at the podium and prepared to return to her seat when a hand shot up in the back of the auditorium. "Uh, excuse me. I have a couple of questions."

Juliet froze. Her eyes darted to the owner of the familiar voice.

"Isn't it true that as recent as two months ago, twenty-four people in Kansas were sickened with cyclospora linked to honey? And only weeks before that, in California, over a hundred fell ill after eating frozen strawberries tainted with salmonella? I could name a dozen more such incidents, all in the last twelve months. I hope no one in this room lets down their guard, believing we've done even near enough."

Hundreds of heads turned to face the voice, likely wondering who would be bold enough to challenge her assertions. But Juliet knew . . .

The voice belonged to her father.

Juliet scrambled for the elevator. She crammed her finger against the call button, then buried her hands in her attaché, feeling around for the pack of cigarettes she no longer carried. Frustrated, she pulled out a half-eaten package of antacids instead, popped two tablets, and chewed furiously.

Like a wrecking ball, her father had nearly crumbled her success on that stage.

She thought she would die of embarrassment, that the audience would be forced to watch her melt into a woman-shaped puddle. Thankfully, she'd pulled herself together.

"Oh, I think we all agree we must remain vigilant," she'd countered. "That's why hundreds of us are here in this auditorium, when we could be out on a golf course somewhere enjoying this gorgeous day."

The remark drew a laugh and took the edge off the tension in the room. She'd successfully deflected what could have been a disaster.

A ding sounded as the doors opened to an already crowded elevator. Juliet shuffled inside and quickly moved to the rear, despite her tendency to feel claustrophobic. A man she recognized from the audience stepped aside, making room for her. "Appreciated your perspective this morning, Dr. Ryan."

"Thank you," she said.

The pedantic man nodded in her direction before turning to her father, whom she'd failed to notice earlier. He wore a slightly rumpled suit, and black frames were perched atop his fading brown hair with a mind of its own.

"Dr. Ryan, I admire your work. I read all your books. I especially appreciated *The Great Hunt for a Sustainable Food System.*"

Juliet's face bloomed red as she realized his compliment had not been meant for her.

Her father thanked his fan, having the decency to give her an embarrassed smile first. Still, her mouth went dry, her palms instantly sweaty.

They rode in uncomfortable silence, stopping at each level to let passengers out. When the doors opened on the tenth floor, her father held the door with his hand to keep it from closing. He waited for an elderly woman with thinning hair to board, then hesitated only briefly before looking back at Juliet. "Well, this is my floor." He gave her an uneasy smile. "Uh, you did a nice job today, JuJu. Your mother will be proud when I tell her."

Juliet raised her chin, locking his gaze with her own. "Traveling without a pretty assistant? That's not like you."

His eyes steeled, his expression somewhere between sad and furious. He opened his mouth to respond but seemed to think better of it. After looking at her for several long seconds, he turned and stepped from the elevator.

The doors closed behind him, leaving Juliet alone with the woman inside the elevator. Juliet responded to her frown with a raw look. "Oh, don't worry. That was nothing. We didn't even draw blood this time."

Before the elevator could resume its upward chug, Juliet pounded the button to the lobby. With any luck, the hotel gift shop she'd passed earlier sold cigarettes.

Order your copy today at your favorite retailer, or visit Kellie's website:

www.kelliecoatesgilbert.com

Made in the USA
Middletown, DE
04 March 2024

50776886R00120